I0731695

BLOOD DOLLS

by Angela Roquet

Blood Vice
Blood Vice
Blood and Thunder
Blood in the Water
Blood Dolls
Thicker Than Blood
Blood, Sweat, and Tears
Flesh and Blood
Out for Blood

Lana Harvey, Reapers Inc.
Graveyard Shift
Pocket Full of Posies
For the Birds
Psychopomp
Death Wish
Ghost Market
Hellfire and Brimstone
Limbo City Lights (short story collection)
The Illustrated Guide to Limbo City

Spero Heights
Blood Moon
Death at First Sight
The Midnight District

Haunted Properties: Magic and Mayhem Universe
How to Sell a Haunted House
Better Haunts and Graveyards

other titles
Crazy Ex-Ghoulfriend
Backwoods Armageddon

BLOOD DOLLS

BLOOD VICE BOOK FOUR

ANGELA ROQUET

VIOLENT SIREN PRESS

BLOOD DOLLS

Copyright © 2018 by Angela Roquet

All rights reserved. No part of this book shall be reproduced or transmitted in any form or by any means without prior written permission of the publisher. Although every precaution has been taken in the preparation of this book, the publisher and author assume no responsibility for errors or omissions. Neither is any liability assumed for damages resulting from the use of the information contained herein.

This is a work of fiction. Names, characters, places, and incidents either are the product of the author's imagination or are used fictitiously. Any resemblance to actual events or locales or persons, living or dead, is entirely coincidental.

www.angelaroquet.com

Cover Art by Rebecca Frank

Edited by Chelle Olson of Literally Addicted to Detail

ISBN: 978-1-951603-14-4

For Paul and Xavier,

who make my world go round.

Chapter One

Bleeders was hopping Sunday night. I tried not to be too obvious as I adjusted the black wig on my head and leaned into Collins, pretending to feed from his neck as a bouncer paused at the parted curtains before our table.

Collins tensed, fingers squeezing into his thighs. The scent of salty sweat mingled with his cologne, and a vein above his collarbone throbbed. I couldn't tell anymore if it was out of fear or anticipation. He was extra skittish since the coffin-lock trial incident at the bat cave, the one and only time I'd bitten him.

"It's clear," he hissed under his breath, urging me away. The peach fuzz along his neck stood at attention, and goosebumps spread down his arms.

"You could have sat this one out." I crossed my legs, causing the latex pants I wore to squeak in protest. The techno-goth disguise was extreme compared to my usual wardrobe, but at Bleeders, I fit right in. Collins' dress slacks and green, button-down shirt had drawn more attention than my casual Elvira getup.

"I don't think so." Collins snorted and lifted an eyebrow at me. "When I sit out on your little side missions, you're not very forthcoming with the findings."

I diverted my gaze back to the part in the curtains. He

was right. I hadn't spilled my guts about everything, but it was for his own good. At least, that's what I tried to convince myself.

Collins still thought my sire was the late Pablo Zajalvo. It was a convenient cover that Roman had put together. Though if anyone up top found out, the broody half-sired stood more to lose than just his career.

Roman's potential scion was his ex and the new captain of the St. Louis division of Blood Vice, Vanessa Sorano. The betrayal could very well end that arrangement, and then the fifty years Vanessa's blood had kept at bay would creep in on Roman in a matter of weeks.

I couldn't let that happen.

I wanted to be honest with Collins, but the risk was too great. My anxiety was not soothed in the least by the lifeblood bond Roman and I shared. We'd been working together for a month now, and just keeping my hands off him was torture. We hadn't crossed any definite lines—yet. We weren't sharing blood or even a bed, but after our tryst in the art gallery at the queen's All Hallows' Eve ball…resisting him had become damn near impossible.

It wasn't love. I wasn't stupid enough to believe that. Vampire biology was a new concept to me, but I was keenly aware of my weakness to it, and I refused to be led around by my pheromones. Roman seemed to struggle with the same problem in my presence, which only added fuel to my desire. Lust was a blade, double-edged with heaven and hell.

If I thought about it too long, I lost sight of everything else. So I tried to push Roman out of my mind as I waited for Mandy to return with the last lead we had on Scarlett—the side job Collins was none too thrilled to be participating in.

The current case we were officially assigned to was Ursula, the estranged duchess suspected of murdering her sire, Morgan, the former princess of House Lilith. The duke wanted us to bring her in. There was an official trial in the works, or so I'd heard.

Ursula was also Scarlett's and Raphael's sire. I imagined she was every bit as evil as they were, though her case file seemed to suggest she was simply negligent.

The runaway duchess had been ordered to create a scion rather than requesting to make one herself. She'd been romantically involved with Morgan and in no big hurry, but the royal family was ready to grow. She'd relented and created two scions instead, hoping they would entertain each other so she could maintain her focus on the princess.

Scarlett and Raphael had entertained each other, all right. Their notoriety was known by everyone I'd interviewed since joining Blood Vice. The royal family had not been pleased by the duo's antics. So the queen had ordered Morgan to create a second scion.

Jealousy. That was the only motive I could find for Ursula to murder her sire. She'd disappeared immediately after, and Scarlett and Raphael had been exiled for their own crimes. They were wanted now too, but that case had been assigned to someone else—someone who was in no big hurry to face off with the psychotic baroness and her loyal lapdog brother, the baron, who everyone seemed to believe was still alive.

So here I was, nosing around in a vampire club where I'd made the blacklist. Hence the wig.

The club lights zipped overhead like a caffeinated constellation. The rainbow of colors faded at the top edge of the black curtains enclosing the booth, and I could feel the bass of the dance music vibrating through the bench Collins and I sat on.

"Right here," Mandy's voice trickled through the cacophony of laughter and electronic beats.

The curtains parted, and Lydia appeared inside the small booth. She'd updated her club attire by a few decades. Tonight, she was dressed in a black poodle skirt featuring a flamingo. Her blouse and the bandana she wore like a headband matched the hot pink bird. She'd dyed her hair since I'd last seen her, too. The once gray curls were now jet-black. If I hadn't been expecting her, I wouldn't have recognized her at all. As it was, she saw right through my disguise.

"Well, well." She propped a fist on her hip, and her eyes

narrowed. "I certainly didn't expect to see you again."

Mandy stepped into the booth behind Lydia, blocking the exit from prying eyes. She wore a pair of distressed jeans and high-top sneakers, but her fishnet top and fauxhawk made up for the normalcy. The white bracelet on her wrist, denoting her as a spoken-for harem member, would keep most from paying too much attention.

Collins wore a similar white band, but Lydia sported yellow—the color for amateur donors. She'd been wearing a red one the night I met her, to indicate her professional status. She caught me staring and covered her wrist, cheeks flushing.

"You brought your harem," she said. "What do you need me for?"

"I'm not here to feed." I folded my hands on top of the table centered inside the booth. "I have a few questions for you, regarding Patrick Nadler."

"Never heard of him." Lydia gave me a tight, unfriendly smile.

"Really? Because he bartended here for several months."

"Bleeders has a lot of bartenders and a high turnover rate. You don't really expect me to remember them all by name, do you?" She scoffed and turned as if to leave, but Mandy blocked her path.

"Of course not." I did my best to maintain a patient tone. "That's why I brought a picture." I laid it on the table and slid it across to her.

The mugshot was one I'd found in the human database—or rather, one that Collins' former partner-slash-brother-in-law had dug up for us since Vanessa was hawk-eying my office research. Before being adopted by Scarlett and discovering that he had a knack for murdering vampires, Patrick's vices had included hotwiring cars and robbing ATMs.

Apparently, Bleeders wasn't picky about their staff. Of course, they also weren't shy about the fact that they had a camera in every corner and a vampire owner who was big and bad enough that even Blood Vice hesitated to cross him. Who needs background checks when you've got Big Brother breathing down your neck?

"Ricky." Lydia picked up the picture and shook her head. "I wondered what had happened to that creep."

I watched her closely as I asked my next question. "Were you aware he was a member of Scarlett Lilosa's harem?"

Lydia snorted. "In his dreams."

"I saw her mark on him myself."

She rolled her eyes. "Ever since being exiled, the baroness fancies herself queen of the miscreants. She'll bite anyone who lets her—and plenty who don't. That doesn't make them harem material."

"Has she bitten you?"

"Why?" She raised an eyebrow. "Jealous?"

"I'm asking in a professional capacity, as a Blood Vice agent."

"Mmmhmm." Lydia looked me up and down. "You look professional, all right." The jab wasn't wholly unexpected, considering her modest and dated costume selection.

"I'm not exactly welcome here," I said. "This was necessary to get past the doorman undetected."

"Undetected? I wouldn't be so sure about that, doll." She folded her arms and glanced up at the mirror spanning the wall above the booth. My eyes followed hers.

Two beefy security guards were making their way across the dance floor. There were feeding booths to either side of ours, but I had a bad feeling Lydia was right. She gave me a sour look and tucked her hand with the yellow bracelet farther under her opposite arm.

"Do you know where Nadler lived?" I asked, desperate for any scrap of information. If I were going to be thrown out on my ass, I wanted something to show for it.

Lydia's nose crinkled. "How the hell should I know?"

"Do you know if he had a roommate? Anyone here he was close to?"

"Persistent thing, aren't you?" She huffed and unfolded her arms to grab her hips with both hands. "Look, I didn't like the guy. I don't know anything about him. And he's dead now, so what's it matter?"

"How do you know he's dead?" My adrenaline spiked, and I stood up from the table.

"You said so. Right? Isn't that why you're here?" Lydia bit her bottom lip. The skin between her eyebrows puckered, and her pupils dilated. I'd caught her, but in what, I wasn't sure.

"I'm willing to pay for the information," I said.

"Oh?" She blinked furiously. "Like you paid for snacking on me?"

My cheeks warmed. "It was my first time. No one told me what to tip. I'd be happy to give you more now." I reached into the pocket of my cropped leather jacket, fishing around for the few hundred-dollar bills I'd tucked away for emergencies.

"You *don't* tip, you dolt," Lydia snapped. "It's insulting. This isn't a strip club or brothel. You do the respectful thing and buy donors overpriced drinks. And you don't drain them to the point of losing consciousness," she added sharply.

"Time to go. Wrap it up." Mandy shot a quick glance over her shoulder through the thin part in the curtains. She checked the mirror overhead as she dug a pair of smoke bombs and a lighter out of her pocket.

Lydia sighed. "Ricky had a girlfriend who dropped in on slow nights. Nicki something or another. She worked at a pawn shop in Fenton, was always wearing a blue shirt with the company's star logo on the chest, you know?" Lydia released one hip and tapped her fingers above her breast.

Nicki. I wondered if she was the crazy chic who had broken into my home to avenge Nadler after I'd offed him at Nigel's party. I hadn't been given access to the case file, and I had no idea what had happened to her after Kai and Vanessa removed her unconscious body from my house. Still, it was a breadcrumb I could work with.

I snatched Lydia's hand and squeezed. "Thank you."

She frowned and inched back a step. "If you're going to make a scene, mind if I get out of the way first? Your last visit cost me my good standing." She withdrew her hand and held it up for me to see her yellow bracelet.

"Of course." I nodded for Mandy to let her pass, but Lydia hesitated.

"You should know…" Her gaze met mine again. "You're not the only one looking for Scarlett."

I gritted my teeth. "Yeah. Blood Vice needed a set of fresh eyes on the case." It wasn't an outright lie.

Lydia shook her head. "I don't mean Blood Vice." Her answer caught me off guard, but she disappeared through the curtains before I could ask her to explain.

Collins stood and stared up at the mirror above us. The security guards were almost to our booth. One glanced up and locked eyes with me.

"What now?" Collins grumbled. Mandy chucked the smoke bombs over the top of the booth before he finished asking the question. Her eyes sparkled with mischief.

"We go to plan B," she said, grabbing his hand.

A chorus of screams sliced through the music, and the crowd reflected in the mirror faded beneath a growing plume of rainbow-colored smoke. It was festive enough to confuse the dancers—but the security guards were not so easily deterred.

I blinked, and my blood vision pulsed to life, outlining the bodies hidden beneath the smog. The inherited trick was becoming easier to activate on demand, but a little danger always helped jumpstart things. With the Eye of Blood, I could make out the larger of the two guards, just a few feet beyond our booth.

It was now or never.

"Go." I nudged Mandy and Collins through the curtains. "To the back," I rasped under my breath, hoping at least Mandy understood me with her enhanced, wolfy hearing.

If guards had been sent to collect us, I had no doubt they'd tightened security at the front of the club. We'd have to try one of the back doors that led into the alley or the adjoining warehouses, including the furniture place where I'd first scuffled with Nadler before either of us realized we were who the other was looking for.

My motives had been clear. I was trying to stop a serial killer and get my foot in the door with Blood Vice. I still wasn't quite sure why Nadler and Nicki—or whoever she was—had been killing random vamplings. I'd pressed Roman for details on the case, but if he knew anything more than I did, he wasn't sharing.

I wanted to blame it all on Scarlett…but the puzzle pieces just weren't lining up. If the baroness had sent her minions after me, their kills would have been more specific. They would have only targeted blond, female vamplings.

I couldn't help but wonder if Raphael or his death was somehow linked to the murders. He was Scarlett's partner in crime. Whatever pies she'd had her fingers in, I was sure he'd had a slice of them, too. Exiled or not, his death would beg some sliver of vengeance. Of course, I couldn't work that angle—neither on nor off the record.

Raphael's death was merely a whisper of a rumor. The few of us who could put that rumor to rest couldn't do so without incriminating ourselves. So we remained quiet, silently pleading the fifth—not that the Vampiric High Council acknowledged that right or any other of human origin—and we let the vamp community continue fearing a foe who had long since been extinguished.

Mandy and Collins reached the back hallway of the club. The smoke hadn't made it this far. We spread out, patting our hands along the curtains draped over the walls, searching for the exit. In a regular club open to the general public, this would have been considered a serious fire code violation. At least they had a sprinkler system. And the sprinkler heads were often located near exits…

"There!" I pointed at one sticking out of the ceiling.

"What the hell good is that going to do?" Mandy barked at me as a security guard entered the hallway behind us.

"Hey!" he shouted over his shoulder, summoning backup.

"Shit!" Mandy grabbed Collins' shoulder. "Gimme a boost."

Before I could stop her, she produced her lighter and flicked it open as Collins hefted her onto his back. The flame grazed the sprinkler, and we were suddenly in a downpour.

Other than looking extra pissed, the guard was unfazed.

"Told you!" Mandy shouted, raking a hand through her droopy hair. She slid off Collins' shoulders and glared at me. I glared right back and ripped the curtain away from the wall.

"I meant check beneath it," I said through clenched teeth.

"Why didn't you just say that?"

"I hate to interrupt, ladies, but…" Collins cleared his throat and pushed the door open into the back alley.

The chilly air of freedom iced the water on my face as we made our escape, racing down the length of blacktop stretched between the club and the next building over. We rounded a corner, heading back toward the side lot where I'd parked my Bronco—and ran headlong into another security guard.

He was a big, meaty vamp like the other two. Of course. And probably older and more experienced than I. Not that that feat deserved a cookie or anything.

The sound of boots hitting pavement echoed behind us. We were surrounded.

The new guard was better dressed than the two who had chased us through the club. Definitely a manager. A gold chain peeked out from under his open collar, and matching cufflinks dotted his sleeves. He straightened them like a grade-A shmuck as he stared us down. His mouth curled up on one side, exposing an elongated fang.

"The boss would like a word."

Chapter Two

"Come on, boys. It was just a little party trick," I teased, clinging to my cover. As a rule, I didn't give up a good ruse unless I absolutely had to.

The man's sneer sharpened. "Boss don't like *tricks.*" Okay. The hooker jokes were getting old.

"Not my boss, not my problem," I countered.

He growled and took a step toward us. My blood vision throbbed, painting him red for a split second before it faded again.

Human. He was human. That was…unexpected. He had to be wearing caps. *The big phony.*

I took the next step, moving closer to him. "Well, your boss might not like tricks, but *you* certainly do."

A touch of fear lit his eyes. His mouth pinched closed, and his tongue made a none-too-subtle path over his teeth, pushing his lips out in a long sweep. Then his shoulders dipped as if he were relieved to discover his disguise still intact.

"You're not really my type, honey." His lips curled back, stretching his mouth into a deeper sneer than before. The fang-check had given him an extra dose of confidence. "You're gonna turn around, nice and slow—"

"Or what?" I laughed. "Are you going to bite me with

your fancy dentures?"

Collins blinked at me, but Mandy didn't look surprised at all.

"You smell all kinds of human," she purred, her eyes glowing a soft yellow.

The man hesitated, but he recovered quickly. "I just fed. Of course I smell like a human. She couldn't keep her hands off me."

"She?" Mandy lifted an eyebrow. "I smell a man—a sweaty, horny, male human."

Even in the dark alley, I saw the color drain from his face. Someone had a crush on the boss. This guy was the club owner's right-hand man in more ways than one, apparently. His faux sire wanted to have his cake and eat it, too. The fangs were a nice touch, and I imagined they demanded the necessary respect the manager of a vampire club needed in order to do his job.

One of the guards behind us coughed. "You want I should shoot the mutt to make a point?" When the poser manager didn't answer, the guard snapped his fingers. "Zane? You in there? We need to get a move on."

"I got this." The manager—Zane—reached into the fold of his jacket. Before he could draw the firearm I assumed he had tucked away in a concealed holster, the sound of a cocking rifle froze us all in place.

"You've got what, precisely?"

A few yards behind Zane, Roman waited in the mouth of the alley. I hadn't seen him arrive. His black commando uniform blended with the dark of night. He'd tucked his white hair under a stocking cap, and though his skin had paled to an alabaster shade through winter, the high collar of his turtleneck and the scope of the M4 hid him well enough.

Zane's brows drew together as if he recognized Roman's voice. "This ain't your business, lawman."

"That's where you're wrong," Roman said. "Once you take it outside, you make it my business."

"Radu owns this entire block. You're trespassing." Zane took a chance and twisted his head around to glare over his shoulder.

"This alley is maintained by the city, which makes it public property."

"What do you want?" Zane shouted, finally losing his patience. This was clearly not the macho show he had intended it to be. "Is this tramp your sweetheart or something?"

"She's a witness to a crime I'm investigating," Roman said. I gave him a pointed look and then darted my gaze between Mandy and Collins. "They all are," he added.

"Is that so?" Zane wasn't convinced. He gave Roman a sleazy grin. "And I suppose a little half-vamp like you is gonna fend off three full-blooded security guards and then arrest a vamp, a wolf, and a human all by your lonesome?"

Roman lifted his M4 and lined up his eye with the scope. "Who says I'm alone?"

One of the guards behind me swore under his breath. "Z, look up."

I gawked along with them, taking note of a rifle tip poking over the edge of Bleeders' roof. Then *I* swore under my breath.

It wasn't like Vanessa to get her hands dirty over something so trivial. And it certainly wasn't like her to let Roman do all the talking. She was a captain now, after all. And a hardass one at that. I'd only been on her team for a month and a half, and I'd already had my ass chewed more times than I cared to admit. If she were hanging back, I had to assume it was because she was too pissed to confront me with an audience present.

I was in for it once Roman got us out of the alley. I just knew it. And it was my own fault for meddling in a case that hadn't been assigned to me while my own case file rotted away in a desk drawer.

Zane's hateful sneer turned back to me. "Next time I find you in the club, you won't make it to the alley."

"What makes you think there will be a next time?" I popped out a hip and batted my lashes. The perfect picture of innocence—well, if not for the latex pants and low-cut blouse.

"I know your type." Zane ran his tongue over his fake fangs. "Glutton for punishment, and I've got plenty to spare."

Roman cleared his throat. "If you're done sweet-talking my witness, we'll be leaving now."

"Sure thing, lawman." Zane straightened his jacket and gave me an unpleasant smile as he circled us. He nodded at the other two guards, cuing them to turn and follow him back down the alley.

Roman used the tip of his rifle to motion Collins, Mandy, and me in the opposite direction, past the dumpster behind the furniture warehouse where I'd found a decapitated vampling just last year. My skin crawled at the memory. I held my breath, recalling the stench of death mixed with rotten fruit scraps from Bleeders' juice bar.

Once we made it to the parking lot, I bypassed Roman and headed for my truck.

"Where do you think you're going?" he asked, tilting his rifle over his shoulder.

"Home, before Vanessa jumps my ass." I stuffed my hand into my jacket pocket, fishing out my keys.

"Vanessa?" Roman lifted an eyebrow, and then his lips parted with a silent gasp. "Ah, the shooter on the roof ploy."

"You mean…"

"It's a rusted rifle muzzle. I'll fetch it in the morning after the vamps have checked in for the night." The faintest grin touched the corner of his mouth.

"Nice." I nodded my appreciation—for his cleverness and the fact that I wouldn't be facing Vanessa's wrath tonight. There was plenty else on my to-do list. "I have a new lead to research."

"For which case?" Roman squinted at me in the darkness pooling around the cluster of vehicles. He'd parked his SUV one aisle over from the Bronco.

"Shhh." Mandy held up a hand, silencing us as she surveyed the lot. Her hair dripped down her cheeks, smearing her smoky eye makeup. "We're not the only ones out here."

Collins rose up on his toes, staring out over the car roofs. "I don't see or hear anything." Then he smacked a palm to the side of his head. "Oh, right, the bow-wow superpowers."

Mandy groaned at his uncool assessment. How very dad joke of him.

"You're riding with me," Roman whispered, his icy gaze locking on mine. "Send your harem home."

I scowled but tossed my keys to Collins, earning a grunt from Mandy.

"I have a driver's license now," she grumbled as she and Collins loaded into the Bronco.

"And two speeding tickets to prove it," Collins said. He gave us a quick salute before closing the driver's side door and firing up the engine.

Mandy folded her arms and then rolled her eyes before fastening her seatbelt. I couldn't hear Collins anymore, but I assumed he was lecturing her on safety. As I watched them pull out of the lot, my stomach roiled with equal parts dread and excitement. Being alone with Roman had that effect on me.

"So…" I held up my hands. "You've got me all alone. What now?"

Roman's gaze swept nervously over the parking lot. Mandy's warning had spooked me, too. I considered activating the Eye of Blood to have a look for myself, but I'd abused the gift enough for one evening. I could already feel the draining aftermath settling into my bones. If I kept this up, I would have to add a third donor to my harem sooner rather than later.

"Come on." Roman cocked his head toward the SUV. "We'll talk on the way."

"On the way where?" I stuffed my hands into my jacket pockets and followed him across the lot.

"To the office. Vanessa's waiting."

"What?" My jaw dropped. "I was just trying to escape a lecture from her. Now you want me to willingly ride off to one?"

Roman shrugged. "Might as well get it over with. Besides,

we have a new lead—for the case we're actually assigned to."

I stuck out my tongue at him as I yanked open the passenger door and climbed into the SUV. "You know, Scarlett is Ursula's scion. They're very much linked. So shouldn't their case files be a joint investigation?"

"If you try to feed Vanessa that pathetic line of reasoning again, she's going to scalp you." Roman sighed and shoved a key in the ignition, lighting up the elaborate dash of the SUV. I had my own fancy work vehicle now, too, but it wouldn't have been very conducive to my undercover operation at Bleeders—that, apparently, wasn't as undercover as I'd thought.

"How did you even know I was here?" I asked as we pulled out of the parking lot and merged into the busy, late-night traffic.

"If I told you that, I'd have to kill you." Sometimes his tone was so dry, it was hard to tell if he was joking. "Why are you so obsessed with finding Scarlett anyway? What do you think is going to happen if you manage to stumble across her?"

"I'll kill her." My humor could be dry too, but *I* wasn't joking. And Roman wasn't laughing. He pushed a button on the dash, shutting off the power to the radio and the other gadgets. We had so much to be paranoid about, it was hard telling what his reasons were this time.

"That would only result in you being executed or coffin-locked. Is that really what you want?" His blue eyes pulled away from the street and pierced me with a look that crossed somewhere between sympathy and agitation. "What do you suppose would happen to your harem then?"

"Like you care." I propped my elbow on the windowsill of the door. "I haven't heard you address either of them by name since we started working together, and Mandy is officially a member of the Cadaver Dogs, so you can stop referring to her as my *mutt* now."

"See, *you* care about them." Roman stole another glance in my direction. "That's the point I'm trying to make. And if you keep involving them in your schemes to take down Scarlett, they'll be tried as accomplices. How do you think they'll fare?"

I tucked my chin into my hand and swallowed the lump building in my throat. "Then maybe I'll just coffin-lock her. God knows that sucks plenty."

Roman inhaled sharply through his nose. "The council decides who gets coffin-locked. First, she'll be offered a trial. What do you think she will have to say about you on the stand? Or about her brother's death?"

Ice shot through my veins. "I'm not responsible for that, and she can't prove anything."

"You don't think so?" Roman pulled off onto South 22nd

Street and followed it past the St. Louis FBI field office.

Blood Vice was set up just beyond it in an unmarked building with opaque windows. In training, I'd learned that the FBI worked out of over fifty offices, and Blood Vice had divisions with more than half of them. What a strange world, hiding right under my nose all this time.

"You're not the only one with the Eye of Blood," Roman said as he parked the SUV and killed the engine. "The queen also possesses the gift."

"So Lilith is dead, then?"

Roman shook his head. "The gift is inherited either when a royal sire dies a true death or when they take their forever rest. Lilith passed it on to Lili when she took her forever rest in the late seventeen hundreds."

"Wait…" Something wasn't adding up. "Scarlett has the Eye of Blood, too."

"You're certain?" His brow creased, and he stole a sideways glance at me.

"She bit me—at the barn—and then just…*knew* who my sire was. Does that mean Ursula is dead?"

"I don't know what it means." Roman shook his head again. "I'm a half-sired from a different house. Apparently, this is one question I can't answer for you." His eyes grew darker. "Put it out of your mind. There is no one you can ask without painting a target on your back—and mine."

"Fine." I huffed. "Then tell me this. What the hell *is* a forever rest?"

Roman made a frustrated noise in the back of his throat. I knew he hated having to add so many footnotes to his lectures because of my ignorance, but how else was I supposed to learn these things?

"It's hard to explain, but it's a voluntary death of sorts. Anyway—" He sliced his hand through the air, silencing the next question before it passed my lips. "The queen has the Eye of Blood, and one sip of *your* blood will do more harm than any lie Scarlett could ever hope to spin."

"Great." I twisted in my seat to face him. "So I guess this is why you've been so reluctant to help me track down the bloody brat?"

"Yes." He bit off the word through clenched teeth. "That, and the fact that we've been assigned to a different case, which you haven't exactly been helpful with."

"Oh, fuck Ursula—if she's even still alive." I slapped the console between us. "She's not the one responsible for turning a bunch of innocent teens into sex slaves."

"Maybe not directly—"

"She's not the one responsible for Will or for me."

"I thought that was Raphael," Roman said, sarcasm building in his tone. "So Ursula is blameless for her scions' actions, but Scarlett is responsible for her brother's?"

"He was working for her." I glared at him. "Make no mistake. If he were still alive, I'd be hunting him right now, too."

"We're not assassins, Jenna."

"Why does the duke want her anyway? After twenty years, maybe it's time to move on. Don't you think?"

"The *why* isn't our job," Roman growled.

"The why helps us *do* our jobs." I pointed a finger at him, refusing to back down. "These little details can make all the difference in a case. I thought becoming an agent would mean fewer secrets, not more."

Roman caught my finger before I could pull it out of his reach. His grip tightened painfully around my knuckles until I grabbed his wrist with my opposite hand. "I'll answer your whys and then some if you promise to keep your mouth shut while Vanessa rips you a new one," he said.

"Why should I?"

Roman's scowl softened. "I want you to take this new lead with me. If you don't piss her off more than you already have, she might just let that happen."

His hopeful breath stirred something low in my gut, and our touching hands over the console were suddenly too intimate. I was melting, going soft in the middle as his eyes bore into mine.

I swallowed. "Fine."

"Promise," he whispered, sending a tremor up my spine.

"I promise, okay? Now let go before you break my finger."

He let go and opened his door. "I'll break more than that if you break your promise."

There was that dry humor again—or so I hoped.

"You break it, you buy it."

I yanked off the black wig and tossed it on the passenger seat as I exited the SUV. Roman gave me a playful smirk as I fingered back the stray bits of hair that had fallen from my braid. I wanted to look presentable for my ass-chewing.

Well, as presentable as a girl could get in latex pants, anyway.

Chapter Three

Vanessa's office looked like it could have belonged to a fancypants attorney with all the oiled leather and walnut furniture. The bookcases that filled one side of the room were packed tightly with human law books. They were all for show, of course. She probably hadn't even cracked their spines.

The Constitution of the Vampiric High Council, better known as the Blood Decree, was a simple—yet strict—rule book. The condensed volume easily fit in a desk drawer, where I assumed Vanessa kept her copy safe from human eyeballs.

While I appreciated the straightforwardness of vampiric law, the absence of wiggle room and heavy leaning toward capital punishment was a bit alarming. Not because I'd become so fond of pushing boundaries—that was totally out of necessity—but because it made me feel like a big, fat hypocrite.

I had my own copy of the Blood Decree. Even though it left the final verdict up to the council, the suggested sentencing for my so-called crimes was not optimistic. It made upholding vampiric law seem like dirty work. Especially when it came to the laws I didn't quite agree with.

Vanessa didn't do much of that dirty work anymore. She'd traded in her commando gear for pantsuits. Her promotion to captain meant more desk duty than anything else. She gave orders and did the paperwork and collected an extra digit on her paycheck. She was good at it, too. I could give her that.

Sharp, green eyes focused on me as I entered her office. It was a loathing look, despite the neutral expression Vanessa kept plastered on her face most of the time. I'd learned the subtle cues of her displeasure. The minute squaring of her shoulders. The statuesque stillness, like a jungle cat preparing to pounce.

She folded her hands over her desk and gave me a once-over.

"The disguise was more convincing with the wig," I said, realizing too late that she didn't care if my side mission had been botched by wardrobe. Hell, she was probably glad it had gone up in flames.

"Sit down." Her lethal calm was unsettling.

The command was easy enough, so I did, claiming one of the plush, leather chairs in front of her desk. Roman stayed in the doorway, his hands folded behind his back like a good little soldier.

"What were you doing at Bleeders tonight?" Vanessa asked.

"I haven't found a third harem donor yet, so I thought I'd grab a quick bite."

"You know you're on their blacklist."

"That's why I dressed up for the occasion." I waved a hand down at my blouse and shiny pants.

"Don't bullshit me, Skye." Vanessa's chest heaved, the only sign that she was on the verge of murdering me. "If I find out that you're still working Scarlett's case, I'm going to put in a request with the duke to transfer you out of state."

I bit my tongue, remembering my promise to Roman. Telling Vanessa that I could do whatever the hell I damn well pleased while I was off the clock would not improve my situation. I'd seen her put another agent through a wall for less.

She watched me, anticipating my rebuttal. My silence was not well received.

"We don't become Blood Vice agents to serve our own purposes," she said, launching into the familiar sermon about duty and submission.

I refrained from rolling my eyes. The lecture would have been more intimidating if I hadn't survived three months of having her sire for a drill sergeant at the bat cave. I felt Roman's heated gaze lick across my skin, begging me to keep my mouth shut. It wasn't something I was very adept at. But I tried.

I pinched my lips together and focused on something else, pushing the baited slurs Vanessa preached at me to the back of my mind. I'd stew over all of that later. Maybe with a cup of Mandy's blood.

I hated to ask the girl for an extra serving this close to the new moon, especially since it was a micromoon, but Collins' human body definitely couldn't handle giving up more right now. I was stuffing him with steak and leafy greens every chance I got. I'd even convinced him to start taking an extra iron supplement, but he drew the line at offal stew.

Mandy had liked the dish. She claimed it was better than stray cat, which I was counting as a compliment, considering how long it had taken to wean her off that particular snack. Although, I hadn't spotted many felines in the neighborhood lately, which led me to believe her fasting was more out of necessity than discipline. Ah, well. We all had our vices.

In three days, the moon would hit the farthest point away from Earth in its orbit. Mandy and all shifters who relied on the moon for their abilities would be at their weakest. The local wolves in law enforcement that Mandy had been spending more and more time with were planning some remote winter camping trip for the occasion. Hibernating in a cave or some nonsense.

I shouldn't have been so bitter. Mandy deserved to have a close-knit gang of her own kind. She'd more than earned it, and she'd been through a hell far worse than mine. Still…it would have been nice to find that kind of camaraderie within my new lot, too.

The only other vamp I'd connected with on a personal level had been killed just to spite me. I couldn't imagine that made the rest of them eager to get in line to befriend me.

There was a certain…shyness I was having a hard time overcoming, too. I was a sireless vampling who drank blood from a cup. The undead equivalent of a virgin who couldn't drive. Ugh. *As if.*

The thought of admitting that to another vamp was humiliating. Certainly not a good conversation starter.

"Are you listening to a damn thing I'm saying, Skye?" Vanessa snapped, crashing my wandering train of thought.

"Yes, ma'am."

Her eyes narrowed. I couldn't tell if she believed me or not, but Roman definitely didn't. He cleared his throat, signaling me to say something more. I just didn't know what.

"I'm…sorry. You're right. I was…impulsive. This is a team, and I should follow your lead." The words felt stiff and robotic coming out of my mouth, but they seemed to appease Vanessa.

"Good. Then you can start by packing a bag," she said. "You're leaving tomorrow night for Spero Heights with Roman. We have a new lead on Ursula."

"Spero Heights? Mandy has some connections down there."

Vanessa shook her head. "I've already approved her vacation time for the micromoon conclave."

"What about Collins?" I asked.

"His last blood test was flagged." She picked up a file from her desk and waved it at me. "His red cell count is down, and so is his blood pressure. He's getting a few days off, too. I can't very well have agents fainting on the job."

"What am I supposed to do about—" I bit my bottom lip and heat flooded my face.

Begging for blood was a vampling tell. Experienced vamps just...*knew* how to manage their thirst. They could go a day or two without losing their minds, and they had connections for whenever they traveled, or for when one of their harem donors fell ill.

Vanessa hiked an eyebrow and frowned at me. "Spero Heights is exclusively supernatural, and it has a thriving vampire community. If your mutt can't tell you the best place to get a drink, then just ask one of the locals to direct you to the Midnight District."

I turned my attention to Roman. "Have you ever been there?"

"Once." His brow furrowed. "It's been a few years, and I was only passing through to pick up a suspect who had sought refuge there. The werewolf on their city council called to turn him in, if I remember correctly."

Vanessa nodded. "Selena Chase. She's the closest thing you'll find to a sheriff in Spero Heights. The mayor, Graham Pierce, is a vampire and a former Blood Vice agent. And Dr. Christian Delph, the last member of the small-town trio, is something else entirely. He sees things before they happen."

"A psychic?" I scoffed.

Vanessa didn't even blink. "Yes."

"I've heard there are other…*things* that live there, too."

Vanessa made a face at my word choice. "The *supernaturals* that live in Spero Heights are quite diverse, but the founders are fiercely protective and more than proficient at maintaining the peace. Even if they were not, you're a Blood Vice agent. Keeping the peace among supernaturals is in your job description."

Heat crawled up my neck and into my face. "Yes, ma'am."

She dismissed me with a nod directed at her door, where Roman waited. A small grin hooked up one side of his mouth as we made our way down the hall and back outside to the parking lot. His face broke into a broader smile once we were tucked inside the SUV.

"What are you so smug about?" I asked, clicking my seatbelt in place.

Roman turned to face me, eyes smoldering. I didn't have to be a psychic to know what was on his mind. He had plans for this trip. Plans that involved me.

Mandy was waiting for me in the kitchen when Roman dropped me off at my house. She'd showered and changed into a set of flannel, paw-print pajamas Laura had gifted her for Christmas. They'd even come with a pair of matching fuzzy slippers that looked like clawed wolf toes.

"What's the word? Are we fired?" she asked around a mouthful of Lucky Charms.

"Nope." I kicked off my heels and plopped down on the barstool beside her. "I'm leaving for Spero Heights tomorrow evening. With Roman."

Mandy dropped her spoon into her bowl, sloshing milk onto the counter. "What? Of course, this would happen when I'm on vacation. It's so unfair. I know that town better than either of you."

Somewhere between escaping the Scarlett Inn and happening upon Raphael as he murdered me, Mandy had spent a month at Orpheus House, a supernatural rehab center for supernaturals in Spero Heights.

I nodded grimly. "What's the Midnight District?"

Her nose curled. "Bloodsucker central. I guess that's where you'll be staying, huh?"

"How do they pull that off without any humans?"

She gave me a patronizing glare. "They have a *few* humans—well, they're human enough. Plus, you don't seem to mind *my* blood."

"Right. Good point." I stuffed my hands down into the pockets of my jacket and pulled out my fake ID and the wad of hundred-dollar bills, depositing them on the counter. Then I shrugged out of the jacket and draped it over the back of my stool.

Mandy watched me as she crammed another spoonful of cereal into her mouth. Her brow creased as if she were contemplating how to best advise me. She swallowed and wiped her mouth with the back of her hand.

"Some of the girls I know down there set up a…café." She pressed her lips together, revealing her disapproval and the fact that the place was most certainly *not* a café. "There aren't a ton of job opportunities for mutts around those parts," she explained. "There's a wolf bar called the Crimson Moon, run by the town alpha and his witchy girlfriend. But they're already over-employed. They took in a lot of the Raymore Clan rejects from Kansas City."

"I get it," I said. "In a little town, you make your own work, and it's easy to fall back on what you know."

"Yeah." She rolled her eyes. "At least the girls are off the dope and not being abused."

"And they're getting paid, right?" I gave her an apologetic

smile. "Any idea what the going rate is for a wolfy latte?"

She barked a sharp laugh. "I imagine it will be on the house for you. You were the first friendly face they saw at the barn raid. They won't be forgetting that anytime soon." Her softening expression told me she wouldn't either.

"Is there anything else I should know about this place?" I asked. "Any weird creatures I should be wary of?"

"You mean besides the bloodsuckers?" She tilted her bowl up to slurp down some milk. "Actually, yeah. I hear the poltergeist at Orpheus House has gotten extra unhinged since the doc found himself a lady friend."

"Poltergeist?" I snorted. When Mandy didn't laugh with me, the room began to spin. "I'm out. No way."

"Calm down. It's not like she's killed anyone," she said. "Maybe gave them a little heart failure or a concussion—"

"This time last year, I didn't believe in ghosts." My voice quivered in time with my blood vision as it crept in around the edges of my sight. "I didn't believe in vampires or werewolves either."

Mandy grinned. "And let's face it. Your life was totally boring."

"Whatever." I folded my arms and scowled at her. "I was a cop, on my way to becoming a detective. My life was the opposite of boring."

"Let's see." Mandy ticked off a list on the fingers of one

hand. "You had no love life. No friends. You weren't even talking to your sister—"

"That was all by choice!"

"Was it?" She blinked at me. "You were willfully miserable?"

"Are you saying that you *are* happy about being turned?" I snapped.

Mandy inhaled a sharp breath. "It totally sucked—"

"See!"

"—at the time. Sure." She eased back in her stool and frowned. "But I'd go through it all over again if it meant being where I am now."

"Really?" I huffed, amazed by her confession.

"Yeah, really. I was homeless and hooked on heroin before Scarlett's henchmen snatched me off the streets." She lifted an eyebrow. "And if I can be grateful for that, I don't see why you're having such a problem with it."

"Because however boring you think my life was, I wanted it. I'd worked hard for it." I slid off the barstool, snatching my jacket as I went. "I have to pack."

There was no way I was asking her for a second helping of blood now. Not if it meant admitting that I was glad for what had happened to me. I wasn't. I couldn't be.

I was a vampire because I'd failed as a detective. I'd failed my partner, too. And now I was here, and he was dead.

Fighting crime—especially the sort of crime Blood Vice handled—was the best I could do to honor his memory. That was the most productive thing I could manage in my…condition.

Shame kept me from appreciating the transition beyond that most days. Of course, the lifeblood bond with Roman complicated things, pushing my gratitude and shame to new, terrifying heights.

Willfully miserable, indeed.

Chapter Four

Roman picked me up at six o'clock Monday evening, an hour after sunset. I'd never really been fond of winter, but as a vampire, I appreciated the longer nights. At the peak of summer, I only saw nine hours of nightfall. It had made for a burdensome work schedule. Tonight would last fourteen hours. Three of which would be spent on I-44 with Roman.

The SUV was too warm. I'd stripped out of my jacket and suit blazer before I realized that had likely been Roman's plan. His eager eyes strayed from the highway to trace my exposed arms and neck. I gave him a berating scowl.

"Eyes on the road, Agent Knight."

He grinned and slowly pulled his gaze away from me. The conceited prick.

I hated that Roman knew how much he affected me. Of course, I knew I affected him, too. That only seemed to make matters worse. My resistance was beyond futile, and with every look he gave me, however self-satisfied or arrogant, I felt my resolve chipping away.

After I'd returned from the bat cave, we'd finally addressed the lifeblood bond between us. Well, as much as we could address it with Roman's limited conversation skills. It all boiled down to this. He wanted a fleeting, passionate affair, and I wanted stability. Normalcy. Some small morsel of commitment.

I didn't need a ring tomorrow or anything so desperate. I just…didn't want to hide from the world. And if I were being honest with myself, I didn't want to share him—any part of him—with Vanessa. And certainly not behind her back. That didn't seem like such a tall order.

So we'd done nothing. Sure, we had to work together. And there had been a few…indiscretions. We'd slipped up and shared a feverish kiss or three. Which was maybe why he'd become such a smug asshole.

"Tell me more about this lead," I demanded.

"All work and no play." Roman clicked his tongue. "Makes Jenna a dull girl."

"You're quoting horror flicks at me now?" I made a face at him. "Charming."

"I could quote other things." His eyes were the color of polar ice, yet they smoldered as hot as any flame. "Come slowly, Eden. Lips unused to thee."

"Seriously?"

"Too dated?" His grin sharpened. "How's this? 'I got plans to put my hands in places I never seen.'"

My nostrils flared. I turned to look out my window and hide my frustration. "You should have stuck with Dickinson."

"They were both advocates for taking it slow. And I intend to."

I sighed. "So, this lead..."

"Right." Roman's tone shifted naturally, no hint of dejection. He wasn't done with me, but he would relent for now. "Footage from a gas station surveillance camera taken two days ago showed a known harem donor of Ursula's fueling up a Chevy Avalanche."

"Who's it registered to?" I asked.

"Benjamin Macaulay. Owner of Nightshade and Morning Glory, an occult shop in Spero Heights."

"Has he reported the truck stolen?"

"No." Roman paused to squint up at a sign hanging over the highway. "Could be he doesn't know it's gone. But if he's involved with Ursula somehow, we don't want to alert him just yet."

"So we're starting at this shop of his?"

"After we check in with the council."

I bit my bottom lip. "Any clue what flavor of strange this guy is?"

"That's one of the questions on the list." Roman gave me a sidelong glance. "Though we'll be more diplomatic about how we word it."

"What did the background check turn up?"

"Nothing of consequence." He shook his head. "Macaulay may be using an assumed name. Or he could very well be old enough to not have a birth certificate on file. A lot of supernaturals don't."

"Great."

Silence filled the cab, hanging between us like a double-dog dare. I knew if I didn't say something soon, Roman would take it as an invitation to fire up his flirting game again. The only way I knew how to dissuade him from that was to anger him or ask personal questions.

There was nothing he seemed to hate more than opening a window for me into his past. It bothered me. I wanted to know him—to *really* know him. Otherwise, it felt too much like I was pining for a total stranger.

I glanced across the cab, catching him ogling me. "What about you? Do you have a birth certificate?"

He made a noise in the back of his throat and looked ahead, focusing on the highway with a scowl. "Of course I have a birth certificate. I'm not *that* old."

"What year does it say?"

"Does it matter?"

"I'm just curious." I shrugged. "Wondering what happens when the *Guinness Book of World Records* comes knocking when we don't die in a timely fashion."

"You'll be issued a death certificate long before that happens. I already have one," Roman said, surprising me. "All of my personal finances and accounts are filtered through an alias with Blood Vice, but once I'm turned and initiated into

House Sorano, I'll be set up with the family trust."

"Oh."

We both bristled at the mention of Vanessa's house. That was the catalyst for our difference in relationship goals. Roman didn't want more to come of this thing between us because he had a future that didn't include me. He couldn't give that up, and how could I ask him to?

I had no sire, no house or old family money. I was nobody. Just some vampling he lusted after at the moment.

Shame weighed heavily on my heart. It leached from me, staining the mood instantly. Roman felt it, too. He sighed and reached for the radio knob, hesitating at the last moment.

"I was born April 2nd, 1946."

"Aries. Why am I not surprised?" I gave him a soft smile. "Are you even a little curious when I was born?"

"October 3rd, 1988." A light blush lit his cheeks when he caught me staring. "I started a case file on you last summer when I thought you were involved with the Scarlett Inn." His grin returned. "How'd you spend your twenty-ninth birthday at the bat cave?"

I groaned. "Hiding out in the base library after an especially painful training session. I didn't see the point in celebrating. I was under the impression that birthdays were too *human* a thing to make a fuss over." I threw a hand to my chest and gasped mockingly.

Roman shrugged. "Some celebrate, some don't."

"Do you?"

"House Sorano only participates in the vampire holidays. They attend all the queen's parties."

I blushed, remembering the All Hallows' Eve ball. "Really? You didn't say anything about Midwinter's Eve. How was it?"

"Boring. Terribly, terribly boring." His eyes migrated to mine. "Of course, how can any party compare now, after the one—"

"Imbolc is in a few weeks," I said, cutting him off. "Do you attend that one, too?"

"No." He snorted softly, yielding to my diversion. "Only vampires and half-sireds set to be turned for the occasion are invited to spend Imbolc with the queen."

I glanced out the window, as much to hide my face as to avoid his. "I'll be at the Midsummer celebration."

"I'm well aware."

We'd had this discussion a time or two. In exchange for saving the queen's life, she'd promised to grant me a new sire. I was to be adopted.

The thought filled me with equal parts dread and excitement. The queen could appoint anyone, anywhere in the country. House Starling in Michigan was my top pick at the moment, though I wasn't thrilled about the idea of leaving St.

Louis.

I'd been living in the same house my entire life. I was attached to the memories I'd built there—the old as much as the new. I felt my mother when I walked through that front door. It was comforting. It was home. Giving that up would be painful, but I'd do it if I had to. If it meant getting a second chance to do this vampire thing the right way.

Roman insisted that it had been a stupid request, but I craved the kind of built-in family he had. A house was stability. It was easy for him to begrudge the privilege since he didn't have to muddle his way through being a vampire with no sire to mentor him. He'd also have a full harem waiting when he eventually rose from the dead.

I might yearn for him, but I wasn't so smitten that I'd lost all sense of preservation. Staying on the outskirts of vamp society just so he could have a convenient, discreet booty call was not what I had in mind. And it wasn't fair for him to expect that of me.

We didn't talk much more for the rest of the trip. Roman found a classic rock station and hummed along to the more suggestive tunes, while I stared out at the darkness the highway cut through.

I missed the sun. Sometimes, if I hurried after rising, I could catch the subtle, dusky end of the day. The fading twilight. The onset of sunrise was harder to manage. My eyelids sagged, and my limbs felt heavy. The fear of not making it inside in time was also a real problem.

Hard to appreciate something that might kill you if you enjoy it a few minutes too long.

When Roman finally exited the highway, and we began a precarious climb up a steep, bumpy road, my skin started to crawl. It only got worse with each passing mile.

Thick, evergreen trees grew increasingly closer, pressing in on either side of us. The SUV's tires crunched over loose gravel where tree roots broke the road, and the thin slice of moon in the sky, grinning down at us like a Cheshire cat, did little to illuminate our path. A low-hanging branch grazed the roof of the SUV, and I sucked in a sharp breath.

"Relax," Roman said, maneuvering us around a tight curve. "Nothing's going to jump out and bite us."

As if summoned, the pale silhouette of a girl appeared in the road ahead of us. I swallowed back a scream.

"You were saying?"

Chapter Five

The girl in the road cocked her head at us while Roman's shaky fingers navigated his phone. I couldn't think. I had no words. I hardly had breath to spare, my anxiety was so thick.

She was definitely *not* human. She was too pale, and her eyes—glossy, liquid orbs—blinked curiously in the beam of the SUV's headlights. She took a step toward us, and I shoved my feet against the floorboard, rising up off my seat.

My blood vision kicked in, and a whole assortment of outlines appeared through the foliage encasing us. Tiny, palm-sized humanoid figures, things with wings and talons, predatory beasts creeping through the tall weeds. They were everywhere.

"Get us out of here, Roman," I hissed under my breath.

"Settle down." He gave me a wide-eyed glare as he pressed the cell phone to his ear. A muffled voice answered on the other end. "This is Special Agent Roman Knight. We seem to have encountered a lost girl on the road in." He nodded to himself as the other person responded. "Yes, she is quite pale and wearing a nightgown. Should we offer her a ride?"

"Are you out of your fucking mind?" I rasped.

Roman silenced me with another glare, and then his eyes turned back to the road where the girl waited. "There she goes now."

My head jerked around, and I watched as the girl flickered and then disappeared. Poof. As if she'd never been there at all. A shiver rocked my shoulders as I waited for her to reappear somewhere closer. Maybe right outside my window or in the seat behind me.

"We'll see you shortly," Roman said and then hung up.

I pointed a finger at the windshield. "That was a ghost."

"Yes."

"That was a fucking ghost!" My breath rushed out in angry pants. I was going to hyperventilate.

"And you're a vampire," he snapped. "Get over it. We have a job to do."

I ground my teeth together and focused on breathing through my nose as he put the SUV in drive and we continued up the hillside. The tremor in Roman's hands as he readjusted them on the steering wheel told me he was unnerved, too, even if he refused to admit it.

Once we crested the hill, the small town came into view. Buildings dusted in blue shadows lined both sides of the narrow road. Decorative streetlamps lit the sidewalks and the handful of people strolling around the town square. A few shot suspicious glances in our direction, and a mother ushered a small child into a shop. I could have sworn the kid had goat legs, but it was dark, so I decided not to mention it to Roman.

His jaw was still clenched tight, eyes wide and filled with a familiar discontent.

"The mayor's office is inside the community center." He cleared his throat. "Dr. Delph said that it's just past the library."

"Dr. Delph? The psychic? I thought we'd just be meeting with the mayor."

"Apparently, the whole council wants to greet us," he said dryly. "Blood Vice has a very fragile relationship with this community. You should probably let me handle the talking."

"No problem." I didn't have the first clue what to say to these people.

It seemed wrong to be so prejudiced against supernatural beings. Especially seeing as how I was one of them now. I didn't feel like it most days. Okay, maybe when the blood vision or bloodlust hit me, but other than that, I still felt more or less human.

I was afraid of the same things as I was before I'd died—including ghosts. I experienced the same nostalgia regarding my home and family, and I was still just as ambitious about my career in law enforcement, however much it had evolved over the past few months.

Sometimes, it felt like maybe I was an imposter. A fake vampire who would one day wake up human again. But there were other times when I wondered if perhaps my human tendencies were just reflex. Were all of these familiar feelings just leftover, mortal residue? Would they slowly fade over time until I was as cold and detached as Vanessa? The thought chilled me.

"Here we are," Roman said, pulling into the dark mouth of a parking garage that led under a three-story building.

I held my breath, waiting for something to jump out at us as Roman killed the engine. Several spaces down from ours, a black Ford pickup was parked between a crusty, yellow Datsun and a BMW with a matte silver paint job. Farther inside the garage, a few more vehicles loomed in the shadows.

I reached into the back seat to fetch my shoulder holster and Glock, but Roman put a hand on my arm.

"No weapons. Not here."

"Yeah, I don't think so." I tried to shrug him off, but his grip tightened.

"If we go in there armed, it will jeopardize everything. You have no idea how long it's taken Blood Vice to build trust here. We can't ruin it now."

"Fine." I jerked my arm free and snatched up my blazer. Before I could open my door, Roman cleared his throat.

"The Browning in your ankle holster stays, too."

"You're killing me." I groaned and yanked up my pant leg to fetch the hidden firearm. I tucked it into the glovebox for safekeeping.

Roman gave me a once-over as I climbed out of the SUV, and I put on my suit blazer. I buttoned it over my blouse and checked the pockets for my badge and cell phone—not that anyone would reach us in time if we discovered we were walking into an ambush. Unarmed.

I gritted my teeth and followed him to the elevator near the entrance.

The eerie feeling that we were being watched tightened the muscles in my back until they cramped. I rolled my shoulders, willing them down from where they tried to hunch near my ears.

Roman pressed the button for the elevator and took a deep breath, that icy calm confidence of his sliding into place. He made it seem so effortless. Maybe, one day soon, a proper sire would teach me that trick.

Inside the elevator, a handy chart detailed what each floor offered. The top two consisted of hotel rooms, which seemed odd for a community center, but I'd seen plenty of other peculiar mergers in tiny towns—a judge that moonlighted as the coroner, and a church that doubled as a courtroom.

Roman pushed the button for the first floor where the chart showed we could find the mayor's office, along with a pool, arcade, and banquet hall. It all sounded perfectly normal, which made me perfectly uptight. A town full of supernaturals shouldn't have been this good at pretending they were some quaint little no place special.

The elevator ride ended sooner than I would have liked, delivering us to the lobby where a dark-haired woman clicked away on a computer behind a rounded counter. She glanced up and gave us a timid smile as we showed her our badges. Something in her eyes shifted more than it should have, and I instantly wondered what she was. I had a feeling I'd be doing a lot of that tonight.

"Welcome to Spero Heights. You must be the special agents the city council is expecting," the woman said.

"Thank you, and yes, ma'am, we are." Roman nodded and flashed a practiced smile, his go-to expression for when we interviewed unwitting humans. It took the edge off his jarring appearance—the white hair and glacial eyes paired with a smooth, youthful complexion.

"Mayor Pierce's office is right around the corner." The secretary nodded toward a hallway that curled discreetly away from a wider one with signs inviting guests to the center's amenities.

"Thank you," Roman answered, and we headed off in the direction she'd pointed us.

The narrow hallway matched the foyer, with a dove gray marble pattern sponge-painted over textured walls. The floor was a darker gray tile, and the baseboards and trim work around the few doors we passed were crisp white. It was a little richer than seemed appropriate for a small-town community center.

"Our annual Cheese Festival is quite lucrative." A man in a tweed jacket appeared at the end of the hallway. His long, gray hair was pulled back in a low ponytail, and he wore a pair of rimless glasses. It was a harmless, professorly look that sought to disarm me.

"Excuse me?" I asked, startled by his random statement that answered a question I hadn't said aloud.

He smiled warmly and held out his hand. "Dr. Christian Delph, head therapist at Orpheus House." My hand slipped into his automatically.

"Special Agent Jenna Skye."

He nodded. "Mandy spoke very highly of you, and many of the new wolves in town are quite grateful—to both of you," he added, extending his hand to Roman next. "I certainly hope we're able to assist with your investigation. Please—" He opened his hand, inviting us inside the mayor's office.

The next face that greeted us was not nearly as welcoming. A severe woman in dirty jeans and a flannel shirt reclined against a wall in the far corner, arms folded across her chest. A tangled mess of red curls shadowed one eye, but the other narrowed as we entered the room, assessing our every move.

Dr. Delph circled us, putting himself in the middle of the office and directing our attention to a man sitting on the edge of a wide desk. He wore a modern suit that looked like a slightly more expensive version of Roman's, disheveled as it was. He'd forgone a tie, and the loafers he wore, while also expensive, didn't quite match. We'd given plenty of notice before making our trip, but it looked as though the mayor had prepared for us at the last minute.

"Welcome to Spero Heights. I'm Graham Pierce," he said, offering us a sharper smile than Dr. Delph had. His handshake was firmer, too. Not threatening, but certainly not timid. A reminder that we were all friends here…until we weren't. The political correctness and casual calm reminded me of the duke.

"Special Agent Roman Knight," Roman said, taking the mayor's hand after he'd released me. "And my partner, Special Agent Jenna Skye." We both opened our badge wallets again to verify our credentials.

"And what's so *special* about you?" The woman in the corner snorted.

"Don't mind Selena," the mayor said. "It's her personal mission to make all newcomers uncomfortable. It's how we keep the unsuspecting humans from overstaying their welcome."

Roman frowned, but he refrained from commenting on

the werewolf's bad manners. "We hope to be out of your hair as soon as possible. We just have a few questions we'd like to ask one of your citizens."

"Who?" Selena snapped. I wondered if it really mattered, or if she was just ready to tell us no and send us on our way.

"Ben," Dr. Delph answered as if he'd plucked the answer right out of Roman's head. Surprised concern creased his brow. "He was one of the first to set up shop in Spero Heights. I'm sure there's been some misunderstanding."

"You're investigating Ben? Ben Macaulay?" Selena's question was laced with a growl.

"Not him, specifically," Roman answered, shooting her a cautious glance. "Someone he might have loaned his truck to recently. It was spotted at a nearby gas station, along with a harem donor of someone we've been tasked to locate."

Selena pushed away from the wall. "There's no way Ben's involved in anything shady. You got a bad tip."

"It was captured on video," Roman said.

"I don't care." She took a step toward us, a vicious, inhuman glow filling her eyes.

Dr. Delph held up a hand. "Let's not get ahead of ourselves here."

"We'd just like to ask Mr. Macaulay a few questions. That's all." Roman tucked his hands into his pockets. I guessed to hide the fact that they were shaking. Mine certainly were.

This woman was no green pup like Mandy. There was a beast in there, longing to escape and slaughter us all. Even with the new moon a day off. I shuddered to think what she was like during a full moon.

The mayor stood and crossed the room. He placed a gentle hand on her arm, drawing her wrathful attention away from us. "It's just a few questions, Selena. They're not arresting him."

"Damn right, they're not." The growl in her voice was still there, still razor-sharp against my nerves. "I'll be supervising this interview."

Roman's jaw tensed, but he didn't argue. This was our best chance. If we refused their terms, our lead was as good as gone.

The woman turned to Dr. Delph next, her eyes searching his with an unspoken question. He nodded in reply.

"Their intentions are pure," he said. Then to me, he added, "Please, come visit me at Orpheus House before departing tomorrow evening."

The invitation hadn't been directed at Roman. I felt my cheeks warm as he shot me a sidelong glance, and I nodded to the doctor. I'd done my part and kept my mouth shut through the ordeal. If this guy was reading my mind and had something to say about it, that was beyond my control.

The mayor's cell phone buzzed from his pocket, ringing out the *Addams Family* theme song. He gave us an apologetic smile. "I really must answer this. Excuse me." He released Selena's arm and gave us his back as he retreated to the opposite corner behind his desk.

Dr. Delph folded his hands together. "I'll send someone to meet you at Ben's shop after your interview. You'll want a proper tour of the Midnight District while you're here. There are several places you can find refreshment and a good day's rest. The wolves you rescued last summer mostly work at Hotshots Bistro, a new blood café, and the Velvet Casket is our most highly rated vampire hotel."

"Thank you," Roman said. I nodded absently, unable to keep myself from eavesdropping on the mayor's phone call.

"Of course. No, hold off on the silver. We'll be there right away," he whispered. When he hung up, the smile he offered was less genuine. "Dr. Delph and I are needed elsewhere. I apologize for rushing you out of my office." He waved his arm, directing everyone into the hallway.

"Is there anything we can do to help?" Roman asked. I guessed I hadn't been the only one with their ears pricked. The question seemed to agitate all three council members.

"No. That's very kind of you to offer, but it's an internal matter," Dr. Delph answered. He slipped a card out of the pocket of his tweed jacket and handed it to me, ignoring the suspicious look Roman gave him. "That's my direct line. Please, feel free to call if you need anything or have any questions. I'm sure our little town is quite alarming for you, but I promise you, they're all good people here, just trying to live their lives with the hands they've been dealt. I'm sure you can relate."

"Christian," the mayor said, tugging Dr. Delph's sleeve. He was desperate to get to whatever problem needed handling. To Selena, he offered one last request, "Play nice. The duke is a personal friend, and I'd like to keep it that way."

She grumbled some noncommittal noise and split away from the pair of them, leading us back down the hallway in the direction we'd come just a few minutes prior. Her purposeful stride made me glad for the flats I'd chosen to wear with my interview attire.

"Is Mr. Macaulay's shop far from here?" Roman asked as we entered the elevator. As if small talk could somehow disguise the fact that we were willingly sealing ourselves inside a metal box with a monster.

Selena tossed back her curls and hit the button for the basement level. "Just across the square."

A second later, we stepped into the parking garage.

"We'll follow you," Roman said next, skipping over an invitation for her to ride with us. Thankfully.

"No," Selena said, shooting the SUV a skeptical glare.

"You'll be riding with me. Your vehicle is too official. It'll spook the locals. Plus, I can smell the silver and gunpowder of the arsenal you're keeping in there. We'll be having none of that for this interview or any other in Spero Heights. Understand?"

"Perfectly." Roman gave her a tense smile. "We'll just collect our overnight bags then."

"Make it quick," she snapped, heading for the black Ford.

Roman unlocked the SUV, and we each opened a rear passenger door. Our eyes met briefly over the back seat. I knew better than to attempt a conversation with him while a werewolf of Selena's caliber was so near, but our unguarded expressions said plenty. I reached into the floorboard, my fingers brushing the Browning in its holster. When Roman cleared his throat, I pushed the firearm farther under the seat instead of stuffing it into my bag like I wanted to.

"You'll both have to sit up front," Selena said as we reached her truck. "Back seat is full."

Roman opened the passenger door and urged me to enter first, much to my dismay. The smell of fresh apple pie hit me in the face as I climbed inside the cab. I'd expected something more along the lines of motor oil or stale blood. My eyes instinctually slipped over my shoulder to check the back seat, and I was doubly surprised.

Two child car seat bases were buckled in on either side of

the cushioned bench. The center spot was narrow but still available. I debated whether or not to beg for it rather than sit next to the hateful woman.

"You have kids?" The question sounded more insulting than I'd intended.

"None that you need concern yourself with." Selena glared at me. The threat seemed more protective than offended, though equally terrifying.

"We'd hate to keep you from your family tonight," Roman said. I sensed the lead-up to his dismissal, but so did Selena. She snorted, not bothering to hide her resentment.

"You're not. Ben's my babysitter."

Chapter Six

Spero Heights was no more than a few dozen blocks clustered around a whimsical park dotted with fountains and gardens. The sidewalks were mostly deserted now, though it was only ten o'clock at night. I suspected that had more to do with our arrival than anything else.

The variety of shops around the square didn't raise any alarms. Everything appeared perfectly normal. Too normal. We passed a post office and a locksmith, and even a cheese-themed gift shop. I recalled Dr. Delph's mention of their annual festival.

On the way over to meet our lead, Selena placed a brief phone call. She didn't address the person by name, and she was none too kind in her request for them to pick up "the twins" from Ben for her. She told whomever she was barking orders at that she'd explain later and to get a move on. Then she hung up without saying goodbye.

Apparently, she was even a bitch to the people she did trust. I considered trying to break the ice by mentioning my own twin status, but Roman spoke before I'd worked up the required nerve.

"Is Mr. Macaulay a werewolf, too?"

The corner of Selena's mouth twitched. Had that been a grin? It was gone before I could be sure.

"No," she answered.

"Vampire?" Roman tried next.

"Nope."

"Fairy?"

She shook her head. "But he does employ one part-time."

I shuddered, remembering the assortment of things I'd seen outlined through the trees on our way into town. Fairies were only cute and awe-inspiring when they weren't real. Like Santa Claus. If I spotted a fat, bearded guy rummaging around in my house on Christmas Eve, I'd shoot his ass. No question about it.

Roman sighed. "Is there anything we should know about Mr. Macaulay beforehand? I'd hate to unintentionally offend him."

"Then I guess you'll just have to be extra careful now, won't you?" A dark light sparkled in her eyes, half-teasing and half-threatening. She pulled the truck up to the curb and stomped on the brake. I had to grab the dashboard to keep from eating it.

Nightshade and Morning Glory looked like the sleepy, winter retreat for Poison Ivy. Gray, leafless vines scaled the brickwork and front windows like spider webs, and frost clung to everything, glistening in the light of the streetlamps. Still, it looked right at home in Spero Heights, sandwiched between a used bookstore and a retro beauty parlor.

Curly, vinyl letters over the glass window of the front door announced the business's name. Beneath it was a list of things that could be found within—herbs, incense, gemstones, books, and answers. We were here for the latter.

As we climbed out of Selena's truck and made our way up the front steps, the door swung open. A squat, elderly man greeted us with a warm smile. He leaned on his cane and tilted his head down to glance at us over the top of his glasses.

"You just missed Logan," he said, earning a harsh look from Selena. She jerked her head in our direction.

"Couple agents here would like to ask you a few questions, Ben. You mind? Because if you do, I can—"

"Not at all." He smiled again, blinking curiously at our badges. They were getting quite the workout tonight. "Come on in, folks. I'll fix some tea." Ben hobbled back a step and opened the door wider for us.

"You don't have to go to all that trouble," Roman said as he crossed the threshold ahead of me. "We won't take up much of your time."

"Are you sure? I make a mean cuppa."

Roman nodded. "I'm a coffee drinker, and this one can only stomach blood," he added, tilting his head in my direction.

Ben shrugged and pointed us across the shop as Selena closed the front door.

Tall, see-through shelves crammed with books and curios cut aisles through the space. Baskets of herbs and crystals were tucked in wherever there was room, and caged lightbulbs hung from the ceiling.

The rich musk of incense filled my lungs. Every step across the creaky hardwood floor added a new layer—cedar, patchouli, jasmine. It was overwhelming. I paused to sneeze, and Selena sidestepped around me, keeping close on Roman's heels.

The table Ben pointed us to had three mismatched chairs. Ben dragged a stool out from behind a small clerk counter in the corner.

"Let me get that for you," Selena said, taking it from him. She wedged it in the space across from the chair Roman had chosen. I took the seat beside him, and we all patiently waited as Ben hobbled around to join us.

"How can I help you?" he asked, grunting softly as he made himself comfortable on the stool.

Roman took his cell phone out and pulled up the freeze-frame image of our suspect standing at the pump beside Ben's truck. He held it across the table, positioning it between Ben and Selena for them both to see.

"Can you confirm that this is your vehicle?" Roman asked.

"Indeed, it is," Ben answered, not a hint of concern in his

voice.

"Do you recognize the woman in the picture?"

"That's Annie. She does odd jobs for me on occasion."

Roman sat up straighter. "Annie…?"

"You know, I never asked." Ben frowned, and a deep dimple formed on his chin.

"Do you have a phone number for her?"

"Afraid not."

"Does she live here in Spero Heights?"

"Don't think so." Ben scratched his cheek with the handle of his cane. "But she passes through on occasion and likes to make a little extra cash by picking up a few things for me in the city."

"And you let her use your truck?" Roman asked.

"She can't very well haul lumber with her *motor-sickle*."

Selena had remained quiet—to my surprise. She stared intently at the screen of Roman's phone.

"Do you know her?" I asked.

"Nope." She gave me a tight smile. The lie was purposefully obvious, and I decided right then and there that I'd save my breath. There wasn't an interrogation tactic scary enough to crack this woman.

"Is Annie in some kind of trouble?" Ben's brows drew together with concern. "Does she need our help?"

Roman sighed and returned the phone to his pocket.

"Not that we're aware of. We'd just like to ask her a few questions."

"Regarding?" Selena asked.

I beat Roman to the punch. "We really can't discuss the details of an ongoing investigation."

She snorted and narrowed her eyes at me. While the look sent a thrill of terror through my chest, the satisfaction of getting a jab in after all her hatefulness was almost worth it.

"Does Annie do odd jobs for anyone else in town?" Roman directed the question at Ben.

"None that she's mentioned to me." His smile was apologetic, but something about it felt…off. He was lying, too. Just not as obnoxiously as Selena had.

Roman nodded. "Well, just to be sure we cover all our bases, I'd like to show Annie's picture to a few more people in town."

"Knock yourself out." Selena leaned back in her chair and folded her arms. "Though I'm not sure how much luck you'll have. Folks around here don't like outsiders, and they definitely don't like cops."

"Are you going to tag along all night?" Roman asked. "I'm sure your sunny disposition will make the process less invasive."

"I don't like the rest of the people in this town enough to care if you make them squirm." Her feral eyes flickered with that unnatural light again. "Though it is my job to keep them safe. So if you even *think* about arresting anyone in my town, I will find you."

She didn't have to spell out the threat. The look she gave us said it all.

The silence grew uncomfortable until something brushed against my leg, and I yelped. A fluffy, white cat purred at my feet. Crystal blue eyes as bright as Roman's looked up at me from its flat face.

"Looks like it's Miss Magnolia's dinnertime," Ben said, easing up off his stool.

The cat pranced after him as he shuffled over to the counter in the corner. He bent down and fetched a can of cat food from a cabinet. The creature mewled pitifully until Ben's knotted fingers cracked off the pop-top lid, and he set the container on the countertop.

"I wish you luck with your investigation," he said, petting the little beast as it noshed away.

The dismissal was polite, but it drew a frustrated breath from me. Roman stood and slipped a card out of his pocket. He set it on the counter a safe distance from the cat food.

"If you think of anything else you can tell us about Annie, please, don't hesitate to call."

Ben nodded. "I'll do that. Y'all have a nice evening now." He glanced over Roman's shoulder as Selena and I rose from the table. "Thanks for the pie, councilor."

Selena's face flushed, but she offered the man a stiff nod. "G'night, Ben."

Outside on the sidewalk, a petite woman waited for us in a fur-trimmed jean jacket. Fake eyelashes brushed high cheekbones when she smiled at us.

"You clean up nice, don't ya?" She waited until recognition dawned on me. She'd been in the barn with Mandy and the rest of the girls from the Scarlett Inn the night of the raid.

"You're looking well yourself," I said, returning her smile.

Roman's blank expression told me he didn't remember her at all. To be fair, he'd been more focused on keeping me from killing Scarlett. Part of me still hated him for that. Scarlett was an exiled heathen. Would the council have really been that angry if I'd knocked her off?

"Jessica Meeks," the woman said, holding her hand out to Roman. She cocked her head to one side and batted her lashes. "I remember your face, too, handsome. But I didn't catch your name."

I bristled at her flirty tone, but I bit my tongue. Roman would only feed off my jealousy.

"Special Agent Roman Knight," he answered.

Selena's truck door slammed, giving me a start. She'd walked around us without greeting Jessica or saying goodbye.

The engine roared to life. Then she rolled the passenger window down, leaned across the front seat, and tossed our overnight bags out onto the sidewalk. Roman bent over and scooped them up.

"Stick to the Midnight District," Selena shouted. "If you feel the need to harass the day walkers, save it until after 8:00 A.M."

"Sure." Roman gave her a short wave that she didn't return. Then she put the truck in gear and pulled away from the curb every bit as violently as she had parked.

"A real peach, huh?" Jessica cackled. "Don't worry. The rest of the town is a lot friendlier."

"I sure hope so." I took my duffel bag from Roman with a frown.

"It's a wonder Ben gets on with her so well," Jessica said. "Of course, that old gnome gets along with everyone."

"Gnome?" I resisted making a face. Metaphors couldn't be trusted in a place like this.

"Well, half anyway." She shrugged a shoulder. "I suppose that's why he lives here with us and not his own kind."

"Right. Makes perfect sense." I shot Roman a sideways glance, wondering how he felt about this new information. His blank expression revealed nothing, which either meant he was on guard...or simply bored. He was so hard to read sometimes.

Jessica waved for us to follow her down the sidewalk, past the beauty parlor, and around the corner. Across the street, a towering warehouse butted up against the walkway. Several bright lights suspended off the edge of the roof displayed a mural painted on the building. It featured notable monuments—the Statue of Liberty, Eiffel Tower, Sphinx, Taj Mahal, Stonehenge—all made of cheese.

Jessica glanced over her shoulder at us and then at the building. "The cheese factory. I bet half the town works there. They keep it running around the clock, so even the vamps have a place to earn an honest living. A few of the girls work there, too. But they still live with the rest of us above the bistro. Can't blame 'em for not wanting to open a vein, but it sure does pay better."

"How many of you decided to stay?" I asked.

"Eight." Her smiled sagged. "Three others left after rehab. One had a family she wanted to get back to, but the other two… I have a bad feeling they were running back to something else."

Scarlett and Raphael had had the girls in the brothel strung out on heroin to keep them compliant. To be honest, I was surprised so many of them had kept it together after rehab. It was a nasty drug.

"I'm sorry," I said, touching Jessica's shoulder as we continued on, taking another left around the next block.

The streetlamps burned a haunting shade of blue down this stretch of town, and at least a dozen people roamed the sidewalks. Live music spilled from an open doorway, a piano and a violin dancing together in a playful tango. Neon business signs stretched over doors and in windows, and couples lounged against wrought iron balconies.

I spotted a man drinking from another man's wrist and gasped softly, my own hunger pinching my gut. A woman seated at a small table watched us pass by. She sipped from a champagne flute, the dark liquid inside staining the glass red as it sloshed about.

Jessica watched us take it all in with a wide smile.

"Welcome to the Midnight District."

Chapter Seven

The Midnight District was not quite what I'd expected. To see so many vampires going about their business in the middle of the night as if it were the most natural, normal thing in the world was…refreshing.

There was a little techno-goth dance club at the far end of the street, and a consignment clothing store with a flashy sign that stated they accepted bloodstained garments. There were also a few blood bars, including Hotshots Bistro, spaced between more mundane businesses that kept late hours—a barbershop, bank, laundromat, and even a DMV.

I wanted to enjoy the sights, but my nagging hunger made that difficult, not to mention the task at hand. Selena had been right about how well outsiders were received. These locals weren't nearly as hateful as she'd been, but friendly was definitely not a word I would use. Jessica clearly didn't have very high standards.

The few people Roman and I managed to engage in conversation weren't helpful. They either ignored us after they gathered that we were feds looking for someone, or berated us in a hushed voice about stirring up trouble in a safe haven.

The thought of coming back to check out the place on one of my weekends off had sounded nice, but if we made enough enemies in our search for Odd-Job Annie, that wouldn't be happening.

By the time Jessica dropped us off at the Velvet Casket, it was almost two in the morning. We still had five hours until sunrise, but we'd exhausted our lead. At least, for now. I decided I'd change into some fresh clothes before circling back to the bistro for a nightcap.

The clerk at the hotel's front desk wore a priest costume. After he'd checked us in, he crossed himself and told us to rest in peace. The keys to my and Roman's rooms were tucked inside little velvet coffins of their own. They'd been handed over with a pamphlet that closely resembled a funeral program, listing off information about the hotel and the Midnight District.

When we stepped off the elevator, Roman squinted at the numbers and arrows posted on the wall. We'd been given rooms across the way from one another. There were two more on the opposite end of the hall, with a little sitting area nestled around the elevator we'd just exited. A vending machine hummed next to a narrow table with brochures and coupons for local businesses. I spotted one for Hotshots Bistro and grabbed it along with a pamphlet about the Cheese Festival and the history of Spero Heights.

The hardwood floors in the hotel were stained so dark they almost looked black, and the walls running along the hallway were covered in lacy, black-and-red wallpaper. It was a little campy, but it wasn't cheap. The place was well-kempt.

I thought of the Cottage Crypt, the only other vampire-approved lodging I'd experienced. And then I thought about Vanessa, whose elderly birth mother ran the bed and breakfast. She was a vampire now, too but, oddly enough, Vanessa's scion. That was some weird family history.

The train of thought also reminded me that Roman and Vanessa had shared a room together there. Not even a year ago.

He'd said that she wasn't his girlfriend. But did he simply mean that she wasn't anymore? She was still his potential sire, so I knew that she gave Roman blood regularly…and that meant he most likely gave her blood, too. Right?

The thought of asking him to confirm or deny these things killed me. It felt too much like an invitation for him to lie his way into my pants. And the thought of him being honest and spelling out what Vanessa had been—or still was—to him… It would crush that tiny, fragile bit of hope I had left that something real could come of this.

I unlocked the door to my hotel room and stepped inside, clicking on the light switch as I went. The place was catalog-worthy. Velvet drapes covered the window, and the corner of the quilted comforter was turned down to show plain, white sheets below. Everything else was in red and black, textured with subtle, gothic patterns.

I dropped my bag on a velvet chair beside the closet and turned around to find Roman waiting in the doorway. The look in his eyes stirred something low in my stomach and triggered my bloodlust. I pressed my tongue into the bottom of one fang, willing it to stay put.

"Something wrong with *your* room?" I asked.

"I don't care which one we stay in." His voice was rough and soft at the same time, and it did strange things to me.

"We?" I whispered out a dry laugh. "There is no *we*."

He backed me farther into the room and slowly closed the door behind him without taking his eyes off me. He tossed his bag on the chair with mine and began unbuttoning his suit jacket. My mouth went dry.

"Please, don't do this."

I'd given up, and I was begging now. He knew I wouldn't be able to resist him for long. It had been murder putting on the brakes the first few times we'd slipped up. I didn't think I could pull it off again. I wanted him. I wanted his body and his blood and just…*him*.

This had to be the lifeblood bond. I'd never wanted anything—or anyone—like this before. This couldn't be normal. How could anyone function like this? It was insane.

"I'm just taking off my jacket," Roman said, looping it over the arm of the chair. Next, he loosened the knot of his tie. "It's warm in here."

I touched the buttons on my blazer, trying to decide if I should take it off. Or if maybe I should tell him to get out more directly. If I ordered him out of the room, if I screamed in his face, he'd retreat. But I couldn't bring myself to do that.

"I'm not interested in being a doormat, Roman," I said, moving farther into the room as I stripped out of my blazer. I tossed it on the corner of the bed and gave him my back as I peeked past the curtains, gazing down at the lively street below. My bloodlust sent a painful throb through my chest, despite the extra distance I'd put between us.

"Doormat? How have I mistreated you?" Roman's voice sounded genuinely hurt. "I've kept your secrets from coming to light. I prepared you for the bat cave. Hell, and that was even before I gave you lifeblood. What more do you want from me?"

"Everything! I want you to talk to me. I want to know who you are. I want to know your past. I don't want whatever we're doing here to be a great big secret. Basically, everything a *real* girlfriend would want."

His eyebrows shot up. "Girlfriend?"

"Well, I certainly won't be answering to 'mistress.'" I folded my arms.

Roman crept in closer, shrinking the buffer I'd created. "Lover has a nice ring to it, though. Doesn't it?"

I sighed and rolled my eyes, but I didn't pull away when

his fingers brushed my elbows and trailed up the backs of my arms. His body heat engulfed me.

"Roman," I whispered in a warning tone.

"Nothing I say will make this easier or change the final outcome." He touched my chin, tilting it up until I looked at him. "I can't stop thinking about you. When I close my eyes, you're the only thing I see."

My breath hitched, and I felt myself leaning closer, but he went on.

"But it doesn't change anything. In fact, it will likely make this even harder in the end. Despite all that, I still want you. Our paths may be destined to diverge, but I think they were fated to merge first."

I swallowed. "Are you quoting at me again? I don't know that one."

"That one's all me, lover." Roman grinned and slipped his arm more securely around my waist. The fingers on my chin slid down my jaw and brushed the side of my neck. "Can't we just...enjoy this while it lasts? What's so wrong with that?"

"I want more than you're willing to give."

"I'm giving as much as I can. You give," he countered, knocking his hips softly into mine.

"We hardly know each other."

"We're in each other's blood. What more do you need to

know?"

"Your middle name. Where you were born. Your favorite food." I rattled off the list, forgetting the more dire questions I wanted to ask. Things about his former sires and human family. Those would only push him away, and I was beyond that now.

My mouth watered for him. My blood cried out for his.

Roman's lips lingered near mine. "Harlow, Boston, and *you*."

"Please," I begged, but I could no longer tell if the plea was for him to leave or to take me.

"You didn't feed before we left the city, did you?" The accusation sounded more like a wish with his hot breath spilling across my cheek. My canines tugged at my gums, extending on cue.

"No. I didn't."

"Good." His fingers dug into my hips, and he pulled me in, crushing his mouth to mine.

I gasped as his tongue dragged against the tips of my fangs, and I tasted blood. The noise it drew from me was nowhere near human. My hands gripped his biceps over the button-down shirt. The fabric was in my way. I wanted it gone. Now.

I worked my fingers over to his chest and shakily removed his tie. When he withdrew from our kiss and went for the buttons on his shirt, I hissed out a desperate breath and ripped it open instead. Buttons clicked against the hardwood floor, scattering under the bed and velvet chair.

An apology was on the tip of my tongue, but I swallowed it as Roman pushed my blouse up my torso. I lifted my arms for him, trying to speed things along. Once I was free of the garment, he tossed it over his shoulder and went for my pants.

This was moving too fast, and yet, not fast enough. Roman leaned in and pressed a feverish series of kisses to my mouth and face and neck as he shrugged out of his ruined shirt. I took the opportunity to unzip his slacks. My hands brushed against the hard plane of his stomach, and when he trembled, I almost came undone.

"Roman." I sighed his name. We were at the line I'd drawn several times before. No, we'd finally passed that point. The boundaries kept pushing farther and farther out. Neither of us had the endurance to prevent it.

"Jenna." Roman whispered my name back to me as his hands resumed their exploration of my body. His breath lit up my skin where he kissed an electric line over my collarbone to the swell of my shoulder, giving me an up-close view of his neck. Beneath his pale skin, a vein pulsed out a frantic invitation.

My fangs extended to their full length, grazing my lower lip until it was too painful to keep my mouth closed. I heaved in an aching breath and then answered the call of his blood, striking with all the grace of a cobra.

Roman shuddered, and then his arms wrapped around my back, pulling me in against his chest. He lifted me off the floor until only my toes touched. I slipped one hand behind his shoulder. My other went to the back of his head, fingers raking through his hair.

His thick blood filled my mouth, searing hot and syrupy sweet. It made every nerve ending in my body sing for release. And then we were on the bed, my back against the comforter, and Roman's exquisite physique pressing down on me. He was all man—from the stubble on his jaw that chafed my skin to the low groan stirring in the back of his throat.

I had my fill of him before my fangs let go of his flesh with a slick pop. Tears of ecstasy burned at the corners of my eyes. I was an imploding star, pure bliss, with no beginning or end.

I laughed hysterically, letting Roman's blood trail down my cheek. He stopped its progression with a kiss before claiming my lips again. Then his mouth moved lower, and a second, more desperate thirst sank its hooks into me.

"Roman." I growled his name this time, encouraging him to keep going.

"Jenna," he whispered somewhere between kisses down the center of my chest and stomach.

It felt like he was touching me everywhere at once. My insides were melting in the most delicious way. Had anything ever felt this good? I couldn't remember. I didn't think so.

Whatever this was that we were doing, I never wanted it to stop.

An hour before sunrise, Roman and I were still lying on the hotel bed. We'd finally exhausted ourselves enough to take a break, and Roman, being mortal, required human sustenance to keep up with the workout I was giving him.

He produced a protein bar from his bag before climbing back onto the bed and flopping down beside me. His wild hair was even more untamed than usual, and a smug grin stretched across his face.

"Don't make a mess with that," I said, eyeing the snack.

"Can't be any worse than the mess we've already made."

I grimaced and glanced down at the sheets. He was right. Spots of dried blood were everywhere. I imagined a vampire hotel would be adept at dealing with bloodstains, but it still inspired a frown.

"We can move to the room across the hall if you'd like," Roman offered.

"No, it's fine." It wasn't like I'd care what the sheets

looked like when I was dead to the world. And if I woke up in a fresh bed after sunset, I'd have to wonder if any of this had actually happened or if it was all just a cruel dream.

I watched Roman while he ate, taking in the lines of his body in the soft light spilling from the faux candelabra sticking out of the wall on either side of the bed. The twin holes I'd left on the column of his neck had already closed, fading to pink dots that looked like nothing more than mosquito bites.

Roman caught me staring and paused his chewing. "It will be completely gone in another few hours."

I nodded, remembering how quickly Stella, Delilah's harem donor at the Cottage Crypt, had healed after I'd bitten her. Of course, I'd had Delilah's permission. And though I couldn't be sure, I didn't think Delilah was romantically involved with Stella. Ever. That had to make a difference, didn't it?

I rolled onto my side and propped my head on one hand, using my other to comb through the tangled nest that my blond hair had become. "How much trouble would we be in if Vanessa knew we were in bed together?"

The question startled Roman, but he finished chewing and swallowed before answering. "I honestly don't think she'd care. We have our past, but it's just that—the past. We exchange blood only when necessary, and she has five other harem donors who have lives and relationships of their own, too."

"Huh." That was an interesting revelation. "What about if she knew I'd fed from you?"

"Well…" He swallowed again, and his brow pinched. "We should probably keep that to ourselves. She really doesn't even need to know that we're lovers. That's none of her business."

"Right." I sighed.

Roman finished his protein bar and turned away from me to toss the wrapper into a bin beside the bed. The light rolled over his muscled back, and my heart froze mid-beat.

A tiny, familiar circle of scar tissue marred the backside of one shoulder. He jerked around at my astonished gasp.

"What is it?" he asked, eyes widening with confusion.

"You…you've been…bitten by—" I pointed at his shoulder, unable to put the words together.

Roman sucked in a tight breath. "Scarlett."

"Why? How? When?" I didn't know which I wanted to know first. My brain wasn't working anymore.

I sat upright and clutched the sheets to my chest. I was horrified and disgusted. Outrage and confusion swirled in the mix, too. To Roman's credit, he did his best to defuse me with the truth.

"Scarlett was my sire twenty years ago, before she and

Raphael were exiled and Vanessa took me in."

"What?" My blood vision flickered, painting him as red as the wallpaper.

"It was only for a few years, after…my first sire died a true death." Roman's eyes welled, and he gave me a pleading look. He didn't want to talk about this, but I had to know. If he wanted to share a bed and blood, he owed me the truth.

"I was already under contract with Blood Vice at that point," Roman went on, reading my expression for what it was. "My human mother died when I was eighteen, in 1964. We were poor and couldn't afford quality treatment for her condition, which I later found out was cancer. I was diagnosed with it just a few years later."

"That's why you agreed to become a donor?" I asked. Something Vin had said the night I returned home from Denver came back to me. *Your blood cures everything.*

Roman nodded. "Being regularly anointed doesn't just keep me young and dashing." He gave me a soft smile, an attempt to lighten the mood. "My first sire had been a noble and a close friend of the queen's, so she found a home for me within the new baroness's harem. That experience is not worth recounting, but I was placed in better hands not long after."

"Vanessa." Her name left a bad taste in my mouth.

Roman winced at my tone. "We were never in love. It was

a business transaction that yielded occasional…benefits. And she's never deprived me for the sake of a brand," he added with a peeved glance over his shoulder at the ring of scar tissue. "Vanessa is fair and honest, and I think I could stand her for another fifty years until I earn my own fangs."

I swallowed the lump in my throat and nodded. The idea of her drinking his blood—and vice versa—curdled in my stomach until I thought I might be sick. Then I remembered Scarlett and the mark she'd left, and the room began to spin.

I wanted to kill anyone who had ever *thought* about putting their fangs in Roman. I didn't care how little sense it made. I didn't care that those exchanges had saved his life, again and again. I wanted to be the one who did that—the only one.

Tears stung my eyes, and Roman crawled across the bed, pulling me in against his chest. "Come here," he whispered, shushing my quiet sobs. "Hey, now. We're okay, aren't we?" He stroked my hair. "We have forever sprawled out before us. We don't need to have all the answers today."

I tried to let his words comfort me, but everything was just too screwed up to wrap my mind around. My eyelids sagged, and I realized that dawn was approaching. In a few minutes, I would die. Right here in Roman's arms if I didn't send him away.

I thought about it and decided I didn't care. I wanted every last minute of this night.

His voice faded slowly, echoing through his chest alongside his heartbeat. I pressed my ear in closer, letting the lullaby of his body see me off into the abyss.

I woke with a start Tuesday night. The sheets beside me were cold, but a note scrawled on a piece of hotel stationery let me know that Roman had left early to interview some of the day walkers. He'd also included another Dickinson line about wild nights.

Be still my sluggish, undead heart.

The blood I'd sipped from him had been fulfilling, but any energy it offered had been immediately spent during our heated union. I decided now would be a good time to visit the bistro. I was thinking clearer and less like a hopeless-romantic-slash-starving-poet.

As much as Roman and I wanted to be everything the other needed, that wasn't plausible. I couldn't feed from him every day—even if he weren't a member of someone else's harem—and he was well versed enough in vampire biology to know better than to realistically want that anyway. Still, I was glad not to have to explain myself to him.

I took a quick shower and dressed in the outfit I'd packed—a pair of gray slacks and a navy blouse. My blazer was a little crinkled from where it had been tossed from the bed, but I found an iron in the closet and was looking professional again in no time.

The hotel room proved even more interesting without Roman for distraction. An intricate cross was carved into the backside of the door, the outline of a coffin engraved around it. And a vase of red and white roses rested on the bathroom counter next to a complimentary bar of soap that was also, unsurprisingly, carved into the shape of a casket.

When I packed up my bag and did a sweep of the room, my eyes snagged on the bed. The rumpled comforter and blood-spotted sheets tightened the breath in my lungs, and a wave of heat rolled over me.

Something tiny glimmered on the floor just under the bed. I bent down to fetch it and discovered it was one of the buttons from Roman's shirt. The only souvenir he'd left behind—other than the bloodstains.

I tucked the button into my pocket as I hurried from the room, hoping a drink at Hotshots would help bridle my senses.

The bistro was more than a blood bar. It also offered hearty sandwiches with a dozen meats and cheeses to choose from—all local, of course. Sandwiches were an easy trade to manage, and fairly popular among the wolves. It reminded me of Mandy, and my heart ached. I'd just seen the girl two nights ago, but I missed her already.

The blood offered at the bistro was served in tiny, disposable coffee cups with plastic lids. It was fresh and hot—and extracted by unknown means in some back room. It seemed too rude a question to ask. I placed an order for a Plasma Pamela, the special of the night, and took it to go.

It was creeping up on seven o'clock, and I still hadn't heard from Roman. So I slung my bag over my shoulder and made my way back to the square in the center of town. I caught several uneasy glances, but a few curious stares, too. A young girl gave me a toothy grin as I passed.

"Bampire!" she said to her mother, pointing me out with a skip in her step. Her mother absently nodded as she corrected her.

"*Vampire*, sweetie. It starts with a *V*."

I licked my teeth, wondering if they were coated with blood. Then I glanced down at my cup, stamped with the Bistro's logo, and realized what a dead giveaway it was—no pun intended. I downed the rest of the blood in one swallow and tossed the cup into a recycling bin near the crosswalk.

"Agent Skye. Over here!"

Dr. Delph waved at me from a bench set against a rock wall in the corner of the square. A fountain statue was erected in the center of the patio, likely winterized for the season. The large Greek figure held a basin under one arm. As I circled it,

I spotted Ben Macaulay seated on the bench beside Dr. Delph.

"Good evening," he greeted me. Then he used the arm of the bench and his cane to stand.

"Please, don't get up on my account." I waved a hand as I stopped in front of them.

"I'm afraid I must be getting back to the shop." Ben smiled and hobbled a step away from the bench, offering me his vacated seat as he dug his free hand into the front pocket of his overalls. "But I do have something for you, dear."

"Oh?" I accepted the glossy rock he offered.

"Bloodstone. Cleans the blood and speeds healing." His thin lips stretched into a grin. "It's not quite as effective as drinking the blood of one's enemies, but it's surely more humane."

A nervous laugh slipped from me as I remembered how I'd tested that theory on the queen. Ben's comment was no coincidence. One of his bushy eyebrows pushed up the mass of wrinkles crowding his forehead.

"Word travels fast, even through this hidden bit of nowhere."

"I'll say," I grumbled and held up the stone for inspection. At first glance, it had appeared black, but it was actually a deep green flecked with a few red dots.

"Keep it close," Ben said, a serious note replacing the

mirth in his voice. "You seem like the kind who could use all the help she can get."

I stared at him. "Umm, okay. Thanks."

He nodded and shuffled toward the crosswalk at the corner.

Dr. Delph patted the bench beside him. "We don't have much time, but I think you and I are due a conversation."

"Are we now?" I dropped my bag onto the patio and sat, scooching as far away from him as I could manage without being rude. If his psychic mojo were stronger in close proximity, I wouldn't be doing myself any favors by getting all snuggly.

"I think you've done enough snuggling recently," he said, giving me a wry grin.

My creep-out factor skyrocketed. I stood suddenly, ready to bolt. There were things in my head that no one could know, and this guy was too good.

"Sit," he said, nodding at the bench. "I'm very steadfast about doctor-patient confidentiality. Besides, I've been in Mandy's head. I already know the things you clearly wish I didn't."

My knees gave out, and I dropped back to the bench. "What do you want?"

"My goodness." Dr. Delph blanched. "You've really been through it, haven't you? I'm not sure Mandy knows the half of it."

"What did she say about me? No—" I shook my head. "I don't care what she said. What do you want?" I repeated.

Dr. Delph leaned in closer, and it was all I could do not to crawl backward over the arm of the bench.

"I want to offer my counsel," he said as if he were offended I couldn't read his thoughts as easily as he had read mine. "That's what I do here. Nearly everyone in this town is or has been a patient of mine at one point or another. I help people. I don't exploit them."

"And what do you think I need your help with?" I asked, still bristled and uptight.

He gave me a strained smile. "Tell me, Agent Skye, how do you feel about vampires?"

"What? What kind of question is that?"

"Do you...*like* vampires?"

I blinked at him, unsure what he was trying to get at. "I guess so?"

"Even though you were killed by one?" he pressed. "Even though your former partner was killed by one, and your current partner was abducted and tormented by one?"

"Okay, maybe I don't like them. At least, not many. So what?"

He sighed, but it wasn't a terribly impatient sound. "Supernaturals who were turned against their will are, understandably, hesitant to trust or accept what they've become. They generally feel like outsiders, even among their new kind, which often helps fuel unhealthy vendettas." He gave me a knowing look.

"I was in law enforcement long before becoming a vampire," I said. "And the case I'm working was *assigned* to me."

"Ah, but it's not the one you'd prefer to be investigating, is it?" He had me there.

"Is seeking justice such a horrible virtue?"

"Justice? Is that what you call the things you'd like to do to the baroness?"

I pressed my lips together and frowned at him. Those violent fantasies had kept me going most nights when all I wanted to do was lay out on my lawn and wait for sunrise. Laura was back in California. Mandy was bonding with her new wolf pack. No one relied on me. Revenge had felt like something worth holding on for.

Now there was Roman. But even he hadn't chased away my desire to see Scarlett burn. If anything, his guarded confession about her being his temporary sire had made me want to exterminate her even more.

"One last bit of advice before you go." Dr. Delph's expression grew solemn as he glanced across the square. I followed his gaze and spotted Roman chatting with a man outside the gift shop. "Don't get too attached to that one. It will not last nearly as long as you want it to, and if you are not very careful, it will end in bloodshed."

Well. That was promising.

"I'm a vampire. Bloodshed is my every day." I gave him a weak smile and a shrug, trying to brush off the warning as gracefully as possible. Dr. Delph wasn't fooled in the least.

"This is going to hurt a lot more than you think."

The smile slipped from my face, and I swallowed. "It hurts plenty now."

"And it will get worse before it gets better." He grabbed my hand and squeezed. "But it *will* get better."

Chapter Eight

Roman and I didn't talk much on the ride back to St. Louis. We were both quiet, contemplative. The tension was split between the uncertainty of our relationship and the bad news that we were on our way to deliver to Vanessa.

There would be no gold stars awarded tonight.

We'd been working this case for almost two months. Every lead had turned into a dead end. Either Ursula was hide-and-seek champion of the century, or we were doing something wrong. My pessimism settled on the latter.

I'd been distracted. I could admit that much. By Scarlett, Roman, my condition—which was still very new and unsettling at times. I couldn't help but suspect that I was the weak link on the team, that we hadn't found Ursula because I wasn't really trying.

I should have been trying.

This was what I was getting paid to do, and if I didn't have something to show for it soon, I feared the duke would decide he'd overestimated my ability and cut me loose from Blood Vice.

I was sure Vanessa would love nothing more. Especially if she found out that I'd fed from a member of her harem— from her potential scion of twenty years. I'd learned the rules of the vampire world just in time to break them all, apparently.

Go big or go home, right?

As we pulled into the office parking lot, Roman reached across the console and grabbed my hand.

"I had a nice time with you," he said as if we'd just returned from a casual date. "We should do that more often— get out of town. Maybe even when we're off the clock."

I lifted an eyebrow at him. "Maybe this isn't the time or place to be discussing this. Vanessa is waiting."

"Yeah." He sighed. "Can't blame me for stalling."

"Might as well get this over with."

"Why? Do you have a hot date later?" He grinned at my scowl. "Would you *like* a hot date later?"

I didn't humor him with an answer. I wasn't in the mood. Not with my insides knotted so painfully that I felt like doubling over. Having my ass chewed by Vanessa was nothing new. It happened almost daily. But enduring it after what I'd done with Roman…

I had a feeling that might be a ninth circle of Hell kind of experience.

I pulled my hand away from his and opened my door, exiting the SUV without another word. Roman reluctantly followed my lead, and together, we filed inside the building and walked to our certain doom.

"So, let me get this straight."

Vanessa paced an angry path behind her desk, her stiletto heels clicking out a warning that sounded like a ticking time bomb. She wore one of her more expensive pantsuits tonight, with a single string of pearls around her neck, and her black hair pulled back in a tight French twist.

"You found the guy who owned the truck she was driving," she said, pointing a finger in the air. "He told you that she does odd jobs for him, but that he doesn't know her last name or how to reach her, and you said, 'Gee, thanks!' and left?"

Roman and I stood just inside the doorway of her office, our hands folded behind our backs and heads hung in disgrace. Vanessa had been silent through Roman's briefing, and for some time after as if she were waiting for him to tell her something useful.

"We know that she goes by Annie and that she has a motorcycle," I said, biting my tongue when Vanessa's laser-sharp glare migrated from Roman to me.

"Great," she snapped. "Wonderful! Let's just pull up the entire DMV database for Missouri—assuming she's actually registered in Missouri and not Kansas or Oklahoma or Arkansas, which are all within easy driving distance of Spero Heights—and then we can filter out anyone with the name

Annie—or Anne, Anna, Annabel, Anastasia, Annika, Anita, Hannah, Julianna, Roxanne, Roseanne. Oh! And we'll have to search middle names, too. And that is all assuming she didn't borrow the motorcycle like she borrowed the truck she was spotted with."

"We showed her picture to everyone who would talk to us," Roman said, momentarily transferring Vanessa's wrath to him. We'd been playing this tag-team game for a few weeks now, buying each other breathing room whenever Vanessa neared the point of eruption.

"You're federal agents," she said through clenched teeth. "It's your job to *make* people talk. That badge you were issued is not something people should feel they have the option to walk away from."

"We were warned by the city council not to make any arrests," Roman said. "You told us not to sabotage the duke's relationship with the mayor."

"And what about *my* relationship with the duke?" Vanessa circled her desk and stood directly in front of Roman. "I told you not to sabotage that one either. Yet, here we are." She glanced down at the watch on her wrist. "I'm supposed to meet with him in less than an hour to discuss our progress with this case. What should I tell him, Roman?"

My insides churned at the sound of his name on her lips.

"It's not like the unit assigned to Scarlett has had better

luck than we have, and she's a far worse threat than Ursula," I said.

Vanessa stepped in front of me next. Her height was more intimidating this close. My eyes leveled with the dip at the base of her throat, and I could smell the expensive perfume she wore. I wondered if Roman liked it. Everything about her exuded class and luxury.

"Scarlett is not your problem." Her voice took on a scary calm that never failed to send a thrill of panic through me. It sounded as if she were contemplating snapping my neck, and I knew that she could if she really wanted to. I wouldn't even see it coming.

I clenched my teeth to keep them from rattling.

Vanessa glared down at me and scoffed. "You might have been a decent patrol officer as a human, tucked away in the tame neighborhoods over on the west side, but you weren't much of a detective, and you're not turning out to be much of an agent. It's a wonder you survived the bat cave. Isn't it?" she asked sweetly.

"Yes, ma'am," I said, the words barely a whisper. I knew that tone well enough to know when to roll over and play dead.

"You were not assigned to Scarlett," Vanessa went on. "I'm done explaining that to you. Don't mention her name in my presence again."

"Yes, ma'am." I tried to be discreet with my sigh of relief as she circled behind her desk again.

"You have nothing," Vanessa said. "As much as it pains me, I think it's time I pass this case on to a more competent unit. Since the duke requested this one personally, I'll have to get approval from him. Then he can decide if *this* unit is worth keeping together, or if the green agents would be better suited for perimeter detail at noble functions."

She was talking about Collins, Mandy, and me. Roman would likely be transferred to another Blood Vice unit. He'd had an impressive record before I came along, back when Vanessa had been his field partner. Now, he was stuck with three agents fresh out of training.

We were dead weight, and he knew it, too. Humiliation overwhelmed me, but more than that, the thought that I might be separated from him clawed at my aching heart.

"Wait. Wait!" I gave Vanessa a pleading look as I racked my brain, searching for some scrap of information I'd missed. There had to be something.

It wasn't just my career on the line, but Collins' and Mandy's, too. And as much as I knew better, I couldn't let this failure stunt what I'd begun with Roman. I wasn't ready to accept defeat or the duke's disappointment.

Think, think, think, I chanted inside my head.

"Well?" Vanessa asked, lifting an eyebrow at my outburst.

"Last summer," I began, picking through every detail, every conversation I'd had with anyone connected to the secret underworld I was now a part of—vampires, and half-sireds, and werewolves… "Arnie Moreau. He said something to me at the warehouse the Scarlett Inn had been operating out of."

"Skye," Vanessa said through clenched teeth. "I'm not going to tell you again—"

I shook my head. "He asked if I was one of Ursula's scouts. Which means—"

"He'd had a run-in with one before," Roman finished. He looked from me to Vanessa. "We should ask him to elaborate on that."

Vanessa considered us for a minute, then she dipped her chin in a slow nod. "The Moreau Pack is a sleazy lot of fleabags, but they don't like trouble. They'll cooperate and even turn on their own if they think it'll keep them out of hot water."

"Arnie was quick to give up names and addresses last summer." Roman scratched his cheek and frowned. "He runs that Cajun joint over near Dutchtown."

"Snake Eyes," Vanessa said. "They do a lot of illegal gambling out of the back room," she added, noting the repulsed confusion on my face.

"Are they open all week?" I asked.

"Shit." Roman pinched his eyes shut. "The micromoon is tonight."

"Then go tomorrow night." Vanessa sighed and rubbed a hand over her face. "But if this lead is a bust, too, I'm going to the duke. I can't keep wasting resources like this. It's even more irresponsible and pathetic than having an unsolved case on my docket."

We were getting another chance. It was a slim one, but it was better than nothing. I was beginning to feel pretty good about pulling a new lead out of my ass until Vanessa turned to Roman again.

"I fed earlier, but I could use a pick-me-up before facing the duke," she said.

I couldn't find my next breath. My fingernails bit into the palms of my hands as they curled into fists at my sides. Then the room turned red, and I saw Vanessa, glowing in all of her finery and superiority, through the screen of my panic.

"I'm Jenna's ride," Roman said, sensing the looming disaster.

She shrugged one shoulder, not even noticing that my head was about to explode. "This won't take long."

"I'll call Collins to pick me up," I said, forcing my voice to remain neutral. "See you tomorrow."

I managed to open the office door without ripping it off the wall, and I closed it behind me without a backward glance.

This was harder than I'd thought it would be. *Much* harder.

I found myself outside in the cold, walking a good distance away from the building before my blood vision finally disengaged. My badge and phone were in the pockets of my blazer, but I'd left everything else in Roman's SUV. I didn't care. I couldn't go back. If I did, I'd end up murdering Vanessa.

Her mouth is probably on his flesh right now, her fangs deep inside a vein.

The thought washed everything in red again until I pushed it away. I dug out my cell phone and dialed Collins' number.

"How'd it go in weirdo town?" he answered on the tail end of a yawn. He was probably enjoying his time off with Laz, but I really needed him right now.

"Can you pick me up?"

"What's wrong? Where are you?" he asked, immediately sensing the fragile note in my voice. I stole a quick glance at my surroundings.

"Forest Park. Near the university."

"What are you doing over there? Did the Bronco finally bite the big one?" I heard him moving around in his house, probably in search of shoes and a jacket.

"I walked from the office."

"Uh…why?" He whispered a rushed apology to Lazlo,

saying that he was being called in to work. The familiar sound of his front door opening and closing followed soon after.

"What the hell is going on, Skye?"

"I really, *really* don't know." I tried to laugh, but it came out as a sob.

Collins sighed, his tone going soft with understanding.

"I'll be right there."

Chapter Nine

"Pull."

The machine set up beyond the open tailgate of my Bronco made a soft sputter, and two glowing, clay pigeons launched into the sky.

I followed the first with the barrel of my shotgun, squeezing the trigger as the pigeon peaked. It lit up the sky like a firecracker, sputtering out in a flash of neon streaks. I pumped the shotgun, chambering a new shell, and caught the second pigeon as it began its descent. Another colorful burst rained down on the barren field behind Collins' grandparents' house.

We hadn't been out here since high school. Papaw and Nanny Collins had a hundred acres just south of St. Louis, and they were both deaf as deaf could be. With their hearing aids powered down for the night, Collins and I could fire away into the wee hours of the morning.

This was good therapy. Dr. Delph could save his mind-fuckery for the locals in Spero Heights.

Collins loaded another pair of pigeons into the target machine and then leaned against the tailgate of the Bronco where I was busy reloading my Mossberg. The shotgun had belonged to my mother. I'd inherited all of her firearms after her death.

"Feel like telling me what's eating you now?" Collins asked, stuffing his hands into the pockets of his down jacket.

Shooting skeet had been his idea. I hadn't found the words to tell him what was wrong with me during our trip across town, but he wasn't about to drop it. He'd convinced me to dig out the shotgun and follow him into the country.

"You look like you need to shoot something," had been his exact words. I couldn't have agreed more.

"What happened in Spero Heights?" he tried again.

I set the shotgun on the tailgate and ran both hands over my face, pushing back the strands of hair that had escaped my ponytail. My cheeks were cold, and my lips chapped so badly that I tasted blood anytime I licked them. The witching hour in January was not for the faint of heart.

"I slept with Roman," I confessed. Collins' slow intake of breath was not from surprise. Until I added, "And I fed from him."

"Jesus fuck, Skye." He pushed away from the tailgate and ran a hand across the back of his neck. "They covered this in the human program at the bat cave, so I assumed you were warned, too."

I chewed my bottom lip and nodded. "He's healed up now, and he insists that Vanessa wouldn't care if she knew we were sleeping together—"

"But I somehow doubt he's in a big hurry to tell her,"

Collins snapped. The crease along his brow grew deeper. "Vanessa would be within her rights to demand repayment in the form of blood from Mandy or me. We could be forced to pay for your crimes. You know that, don't you?"

"I'm sorry. I shouldn't have—"

"No, you shouldn't have," he echoed. "Do you have any idea how helpless I feel when it comes to my own future now?"

"Collins…" My shame was already spread thin, but it stretched a little further at his words.

"I'm the bottom of the barrel as far as Blood Vice is concerned. I'm viewed as nothing more than an extension of you, and since I'm not half-sired or supernatural, I'm basically a glorified blood bag. Fang fodder—that's what they call me behind my back."

I shook my head. "I didn't know. I'm sorry."

"I didn't tell you because I didn't want you to feel bad." He scoffed. "But here you are, snacking on someone else's harem—on our *boss's* harem—not giving two shits about those who will suffer for your actions when I'd gladly open a vein for you. And I have, countless times."

"Too many times." I knew Collins had seen the results of his last physical by now.

He glared at me. "That's no excuse. There are legitimate ways to fill the gap in your *diet*."

"Yeah." I winced at the accusation. "I'm working on it."

"Do you know what the other agents say about *you*?" He was still full of venom, and I deserved every bit of it. "You realize that they think you're the duke's Achilles' heel? Some suspect you're his mistress, and others think you're only with the agency because you're blackmailing him. There are even worse…" His voice dropped lower, and he shot a nervous glance out across the field. The floodlights off the back of his grandparents' house reached all the way to the shadows clinging to the tree line on the opposite side. "There are rumors that the exiled baron is dead, and that you're to blame."

My breath ached in my lungs, and I couldn't find the nerve to lie to Collins' face. I stared at him, knowing each second that passed was another nail in my coffin.

"Are you, Skye?" he whispered. "Is Blood Vice just a convenient resource to help you pick off your next royal target?" I couldn't tell if he was being serious or just mocking me now.

"I saved the queen's life," I reminded him.

"Something tells me you wouldn't extend that same courtesy to Scarlett or Ursula." He swallowed and looked out over the field again. "And if you're in this mess as deep as I think you are, where does that leave me, your fragile, expendable blood slave?"

"Collins, that's not what you are to me, and you know it." I sighed and reached into the bed of the Bronco to grab my shotgun case. I didn't feel like shooting anymore. I felt like *being* shot. Maybe that would sap out some of this guilt weighing me down.

"I can't speak for Mandy, but your stunt with Roman puts her in the line of fire, too." Collins gave me a hard look. "She deserves to know that."

"Yeah." I snorted. "I'll be sure to drop that bomb on her just as soon as she gets back from her camping trip."

Collins gathered up the box of pigeons and carried it over to his Toyota. After he'd packed up the machine and I'd picked up the spent shells littering the ground, he met me at the tailgate of the Bronco again.

"I don't know if you heard or not," he said, looking only slightly less vindictive. "Patz is retiring in March."

Patz was the killjoy sergeant who ran the patrol division Collins and I had both served on. It seemed an odd thing to suddenly bring up. It wasn't like we'd be getting invitations to the retirement party.

"So?" I said.

Collins shrugged. "Ramirez will be filling his spot. We talked about it over Christmas, and he asked if I'd ever consider coming back. Said he could hook me up with dayshift."

"Oh." Guilt sucker-punched me again.

Joining Blood Vice with me hadn't done Collins' home life any favors. The three months in Denver had put enough strain on his marriage. Add in the nightshift he'd begun working once we returned, and it was no wonder Lazlo's brother was throwing Collins a bone.

"Maybe you should take him up on that," I said, praying my sincerity came through more than my bitterness. "I'm dangerous to be around. I get it, really—"

"You *make* yourself dangerous to be around," Collins said. He gave me a pitying look, but he wasn't pulling any punches tonight. "You always have. It pushes people away—people who care about you. I'm trying so hard to be a good friend, but you don't make it easy."

"I know. I know."

There was nothing else I could offer. I thought we'd come out here so I could get something off my chest, but it looked like Collins was just as badly in need of that. And he *was* a good friend—a far better friend than I'd been in return.

What was I doing with my life? The question felt like one I'd been trying to answer ever since my mother died. For the longest time, I was positive I wanted to be just like her. But I was so far off that path now. That life was over.

Collins turned away from me and circled the Toyota to the driver's side without saying goodbye. He wasn't exactly storming off, but he wasn't taking back anything he'd said either. He meant it all. And now that he'd spoken his piece, only a hollow sadness remained between us.

I swallowed and blinked away a tear, blaming it on the cold wind sweeping across the field. Then I climbed inside the Bronco and went home.

Mandy wouldn't be returning from her camping trip until Thursday morning. I'd lived alone in my house for nearly ten years before she came crashing into my world, and now I could hardly stand the silence when she wasn't around.

But silence wasn't something I had to worry about tonight, I realized as I pulled into my driveway and spotted Roman's SUV parked at the curb. He sat on the front steps of my porch, arms folded over his knees.

"What are you doing here?" I slammed the door of the Bronco and took a few careful steps in his direction. Maybe this would be easier if I didn't stand so close to him.

Roman nodded behind him at my duffel bag, resting in the wicker chair under the porch light. "You forgot your overnight bag." The reply sounded innocent enough, but when he stood and moved toward me, I froze in the middle of the sidewalk. Roman paused and gave me a peculiar look.

"Thanks." My throat went dry before I could add "goodnight." That would have been the right thing to say to him.

My eyes fixed on the side of Roman's neck where I'd bitten him the night before. I wondered if Vanessa had chosen the same spot or somewhere else. There were so many succulent stretches of skin to choose from. My mouth had found them all, taking inventory for future reference—as if we had a future.

Shame touched Roman's cheeks as he realized where and why I was staring. He rolled his head to one side, popping his neck, and then cleared his throat.

"I've been waiting awhile. Where were you?" An unmistakable note of jealousy stained his voice.

"With Collins." I didn't have it in me to lie to him.

Making Roman as ugly jealous as I was wouldn't help anything, and this wasn't his fault. He couldn't just leave Vanessa. It was part of his contract with Blood Vice. And if she stopped anointing him, it wasn't like I could take over that responsibility. Not legally. It would be at least another fifty years before House Lilith would even *consider* letting me half-sire a human donor.

There was a healthy chance that Roman was right and Vanessa would, in fact, not care that we had slept together. Or, at least, she wouldn't care enough to kill us over it. In some strange act of generosity or gratitude, say, maybe if we managed to find Ursula, I could even see her giving us her blessing.

But one thing she would never condone was Roman giving his blood to me. And even more than sex, that's what I wanted from him. I could tell that's what he wanted from me, too. After our latest tryst, how could we settle for anything less?

There was no way this could go on without us breaking the rules, but the fact that we'd broken so many already and had gotten away with it made us bold. I was well aware of that. From my earliest missteps as a rogue vampling to my carefully constructed sire cover-up. But our luck had to run out at some point.

"That was a good lead you came up with tonight," Roman said, breaking the awkward silence.

"Yeah, we'll see."

"Mandy home?" He glanced up at the darkened front window.

"Not for another day."

"Four hours till sunrise."

My breath rushed out. "And?"

"And?" Roman laughed and gave me a wry grin. "What do you think?"

"I think you shouldn't be offering up your blood twice in

one night, and certainly not right before we have a date with a pack of wild dogs." I stepped into the lawn and darted around him, heading for the porch, but he caught my wrist.

"What if we skip the blood?" he asked, strain tightening his voice.

"I don't think I can do that." I shook my head. "It's a bad idea."

I thought of the blood I'd had earlier in the evening at Hotshots. It was enough to keep me going, just like Mandy and Collins kept me going, but that hunger was always there. The only time it had come close to being satisfied was at the bat cave when I'd had four donors working in rotation.

"What if I tie you up?" Roman asked next. "What if you were to drink a cup from one of your harem first?"

"What if, what if, what if." I sighed, trying to add more solution to our problem than resistance. "What if we wait until this case pans out? What if we wait until I have a third or fourth donor?"

Roman's grip on my wrist tightened at the mention of adding donors. "What about that woman you drank from at Bleeders?"

"What about her?"

"She seemed nice," he said. "You could solicit her—though she was a little excitable. Maybe she'd be willing to bleed in a cup like Mandy and Collins."

"Do you bleed in a cup for Vanessa?" I asked, unable to hide my irritation.

"I would if she'd accept that." He tugged at my wrist, pulling me around to face him. "You know I would."

I sighed and closed my eyes. "We can't do this right now. It's too risky, and I have to think about Mandy and Collins. I can't be selfish."

Roman's hands slid up my arms, and he panted out a heavy breath as he leaned into me. "I'll sneak you into Bleeders. Tonight. You can have your fill, and then I'll tie you to the bed." His mouth brushed my temple and then dipped down to the top of one ear.

"This is ridiculous," I hissed at him, unable to hide the smile creeping over my face. "I can't go to Bleeders. I'm on the blacklist. Even if the guards don't spot me, Lydia will, and she's in enough trouble because of me as it is—" I sucked in a ragged breath and nudged Roman away. "Lydia."

"Try *lover*," he said, pulling me closer, but I kept a firm hand on his chest.

"She said I wasn't the only one looking for Scarlett." I blinked at Roman.

"I'm sure the agents assigned to the case didn't overlook Bleeders."

"She said it wasn't Blood Vice."

Roman finally stopped fondling me long enough to

consider what I'd said. "You think…?"

"What if Annie is the same scout Ursula sent to look for Scarlett?" I asked.

"And what if she stopped in at Bleeders along the way?"

My hands softened on his chest now that I didn't have to fend him off. He valued his career, too. Probably even more than I did. He wouldn't let a viable lead rot over our personal turmoil.

"Blood Vice hacked Bleeders' security footage last summer," I said. "Think we could do that again?"

"And scour through it for motorcycle Annie?" Roman frowned. "That could take some time."

"What do we have to lose? You know, besides everything."

Chapter Ten

The image we had of Annie from the gas station wasn't spectacular, but it was clear enough to get an objective look at her. She was attractive. In a normal, dismissible way.

Her brunette hair hung in soft waves just past her jawline, and snug jeans served to draw more attention to her ass than her face. At least a thousand women who could have passed for her came in and out of Bleeders every night. Seven nights a week.

The security feed Blood Vice's tech team hacked into only went back three weeks. We could start there, but anything beyond that would require a warrant—or a more elaborate heist than we had time for.

As it was, we hadn't even called Vanessa to tell her about this new, shot-in-the-dark lead we were pursuing. She was still at her meeting with the duke, for which I was glad. I wasn't ready to face her yet. Not after how much effort it had taken to get away from her earlier without going off like an atomic bomb.

The building Blood Vice worked out of in St. Louis was fairly small. Vanessa had a nice corner office, but the dozen or so units that worked under her roof hardly had a square of cubical space each to call their own. It was a matter of security rather than budget restraints, and the SUVs with all the bells and whistles mostly made up for it.

There was a swanky tech lab on the opposite side of the building from Vanessa's office, with the sad cubical floor spanning between the two. A supernatural morgue and an evidence lab took up most of the basement, all except for two quarantine holding cells tucked behind the stairwell. They were soundproof and reinforced with concrete that had been mixed through with silver. If a special *guest* attempted to punch their way through a wall, they wouldn't make it far before passing out from the toxic dust.

A vampire named Phil let Roman and me into the tech lab. It was a quiet space I'd never seen occupied by more than an agent or two at a time. Tonight, it was just Phil. He set us up at a pair of widescreen computers and gave a quick crash course on how to work the video controls. Then he tapped into Bleeders' security network.

Roman took the recordings gathered from the feed in the back alley, and I took the camera pointed at the front parking lot. The plan was to first examine anyone who arrived via motorcycle. But Vanessa was right. Annie could have easily borrowed any number of vehicles.

It was a tedious task—picking through security footage, pausing, zooming in and out, swearing, and moving on—but it felt constructive. And it kept us busy through the dark leading up to dawn.

There were so many other things that I wanted to be doing—that I was sure Roman wanted to be doing, too. The small victory of doing my job over doing him would have been more gratifying if we'd actually found something.

I cut it close, breaking off half an hour before sunrise. Roman offered to drive me home, but I waved for him to stay put at his screen.

"Keep looking as long as you're able," I said, buttoning my blazer. "I'll be back here just as soon as the sun sets. You should call Collins in to help."

Roman frowned, but he nodded without asking why I hadn't made the suggestion sooner or called myself. Truthfully, I wasn't even sure Collins would pick up if he saw my name on his caller ID.

"Shoot a text to let me know you made it home in time," he said, turning back to his screen as if he hadn't just made a very relationship-y request of me.

"Sure."

I slipped out of the office and climbed inside the Bronco. My work SUV was still tucked away in the garage at my house where I'd parked it before Roman and I had left for Spero Heights. It would stay there tonight too, since I'd likely be riding along with Roman when we went to see Arnie in Dutchtown.

I hurried across the city and pulled into my driveway with

ten minutes to spare. I texted Roman a simple *home,* and still had enough time to check the mail and brush my teeth. Afterward, I collapsed on my bed, willing the sun to hurry its trajectory across the sky. I had shit to do.

I can sleep when I'm dead, I thought.

Then I blinked and was.

I dreamt of Roman and Spero Heights, but the sensual memory was riddled with flashes of Vanessa and Scarlett, spinning the scene away into commercial breaks of violent, vengeful fantasies.

They wove together through my mindscape, lust and wrath and envy, all dripping with blood until I couldn't tell them apart. They were one.

The same blood with a kaleidoscope of flavors.

And I wanted them all.

Roman was exhausted and grouchy when I met up with him again Wednesday night. His suit looked familiar, as if maybe it could have been the same one he'd been wearing that morning. Though his conservative, forgettable work attire was all so similar, I couldn't be certain.

I'd always been more interested in what lay beneath.

After my involuntary ten hours of rest, I'd woken with a shuddering gasp at sunset, my body covered in sweat. Not even a cold shower could shake the images of the adventures I'd had behind closed eyes.

My mouth was impossibly dry, and my stomach roiled at the sight of Roman. I needed to feed soon.

Mandy wouldn't be back for several hours, and Collins looked ready to keel over at the computer screen I'd been stationed in front of that morning. He glanced up and gave me a curt nod.

Roman stood and yawned into his closed fist. "Nothing yet," he answered before I could ask. "But we still have a week's worth to comb through. I'm going to choke down a cup of coffee, and then we can get going."

I nodded as he left the tech lab and double-checked the Glock in the holster hidden under my blazer. Then I checked the Browning in the ankle holster under my slacks and readjusted my ponytail.

The mindless activity helped distract me from the stiff line of Collins' back. He was waiting for me to request blood from him. I wanted to, and I really should have, but I just couldn't. Not after everything he'd said at his grandparents' place.

It could wait, I convinced myself. I'd gone for longer than this without blood and had been just fine. Mandy would be home in the morning. She'd promised to return before sunrise. The only side effect I'd have to deal with until then was being a little bitchier than usual—which I wasn't really worried about, considering where the night would lead us.

Roman returned and rapped his knuckles against Collins' desk. "Why don't you grab a bite to eat and then get back at it? Call if you find anything."

Collins nodded, but he didn't look up from the computer screen or say anything as we left. The subtle rub didn't escape Roman's attention. Once we loaded into his SUV, he let me have it.

"What does he know?" he asked. It took three tries before he finally managed to cram his key into the ignition.

"Nothing." I shook my head. "Did you get *any* sleep today? Should I be driving?"

"*What* does he know, Jenna?"

I sighed and met his gaze. Even rough around the edges, he was devastating. "Collins deserves to know," I said.

Roman's jaw flexed. He swallowed and turned away from me to glare out the windshield. "Who else deserves to know? Mandy? Vanessa maybe? Would you like to call her and spill your guts next?"

"Don't worry about Collins." I fastened my seatbelt as he backed out of the parking lot. "He'll be putting in his notice soon enough, and then I'll have a second harem opening to fill."

The SUV bumped over the curb, and Roman mumbled a gruff apology. The mention of my harem agitated him the way being reminded of Vanessa agitated me. We kept rubbing salt into each other's wounds. Maybe it had been unintentional at first, but I could see how this might escalate.

The drive to Dutchtown was a short one, but it felt like forever with Roman giving me the cold shoulder. He didn't ask why Collins was leaving, and I didn't offer up any more details. I was sure he was clever enough to put the pieces together on his own.

It was right around dinnertime when we arrived at Snake Eyes, but the block the building slouched in the middle of was nearly deserted. The check-cashing business and pawnshop across the street had *Closed* signs hanging in their doors and bars over their windows.

A car on blocks took up three spaces of the parking lot wedged between the restaurant and a boarded-up building. Weeds grew up through the gravel to tickle the sagging bumpers, and a scrawny cat darted underneath it as Roman pulled in. It looked like most of the guests at Snake Eyes preferred two wheels. A row of motorcycles crowded behind a railing that enclosed a patch of cracked pavement. The space was probably used as an outdoor patio during the warmer months.

Roman claimed the remaining two spaces of the parking lot, clicking off the headlights prematurely so they wouldn't flash through a side window. The element of surprise was always a plus. We climbed out of the SUV and stepped lightly on our way up to the front entrance, past the motorcycles and an overflowing ashtray tower.

Snake Eyes was less Cajun restaurant and more hole-in-the-wall biker bar. The place reeked of stale beer and rancid fish. A row of three vacant booths rested against one wall. The cracked, vinyl seats had been repaired with duct tape, and a stack of stained menus was wedged between bottles of hot sauce and novelty jars of pickled reptiles.

Two billiards tables filled most of the remaining floor space, with several pub tables scattered along the wall opposite the booths and a long bar angled in the back corner. A jukebox blasted a gravelly Kid Rock song that fought to be heard over a boxing match playing on a television behind the counter.

The only soul in sight was a bald man in a hooded sweatshirt. A tattoo of a cobra curled up one side of his head, and a thick ring hung from his nostrils. His attention was focused more on the fight than the bottles of booze he was restocking at the bar well. He didn't hear Roman and me come in, which immediately made me think *human*. We would have never gotten the drop on a werewolf so easily.

I followed Roman's silent lead, taking long strides right through the place like we owned it. A swinging door led into a kitchen just beyond the bar. The bartender watching the fight didn't notice us until we'd pushed past it, leaving him to shout at our backs.

The kitchen was quiet except for a sizzling, unattended fryer we passed on our way through to a second swinging door that led to a back room. Muffled laughter and cheap tobacco smoke greeted us as we curled around a walk-in cooler and past a rolling shelf that held moldy tomatoes and an open sack of rice. It was darker here than in the kitchen, with concrete walls that seemed to swallow the stark light coming from a long, florescent fixture overhead.

Three men sat around a table playing cards. They each wore a leather jacket with the pack's faded insignia stamped into the backside. Beer bottles and ashtrays were spaced between them, leaving room for their meager kitty in the center. They didn't fall over themselves when they saw us, but the smiles slipped from their faces, and they sat up straighter.

It had been a while since I'd crossed paths with Arnie Moreau. Mandy and I had bumped into him at the abandoned Scarlett Inn after she'd chased one of his goons through the building. We'd had ourselves a good, old-fashioned standoff until Roman arrived to tip the odds in my favor—though he'd arrested Arnie and kept me from questioning him further about where the girls from the inn were.

Arnie had sung like a canary for Blood Vice, and was pardoned for his cooperation. Before that, though, he had promised me that he'd make bail, and that we would have a *good time* when he did. Considering his motives for seeking out the Scarlett Inn in the first place, the threat had painted a graphic picture. His face was locked away in my vault of unredeemable evils.

"Well, look who it is?" His beady eyes sparkled as they took me in. "I wondered when I'd see you again, sweetheart."

The bald bartender paused a few steps behind Roman and me. "I'm sorry, boss. They just barged in and slipped right by me—" Arnie cut him off with a sharp jerk of his chin.

"Get back out front and do your job for a change," he barked. The man dipped his head apologetically and hurried back around the walk-in cooler and through the swinging door.

Roman cleared his throat. "Word on the street is you had a run-in with one of Ursula's scouts, Arnie."

"Oh, I have run-ins with lots of feisty bitches." He waggled an eyebrow at me.

"We're going to need a description of her, what she was driving, and where this meeting took place," Roman said.

Arnie sniffed and ignored the question, turning his attention to me again. "Where's your sidekick? Did the little wolf girl run off to join her pack of whores down in Spero Heights?" He laughed at my surprise. "She was my brother's favorite. Did you know? Did she ever tell you about all the fun he had with her?"

The walls pulsed around me. The room turned red and constricted as if we were trapped within a thundering heart. He was trying to distract me from what we'd come for, trying to push new questions into my head—ones he thought I'd be willing to beg for.

How did he know about Spero Heights? Where was Marcel hiding? How could I find that bastard, and how many ways could I make him bleed?

"Careful, Arnie," Roman warned. "She hasn't fed tonight."

The wolf pushed back from the table and stood. He glanced at his hand of cards and then threw them facedown on the table. His jacket gaped, showing the handle of a pistol hooked into the waistband of his jeans.

Roman drew his sidearm, but he kept it aimed at the floor. He didn't want this to get messy. Messy wasted time that we didn't have.

Arnie eyed him cautiously, even as his crooked grin widened, creating twin dimples on either side of his mouth. He brushed a hand through his greasy slick of hair and circled the table, stalking closer to us. My blood vision throbbed in time with his every step.

He stopped a few feet in front of me, as if I were on display for him and he wanted a closer look. It was a show of power for his pack. Their comfort seemed to improve the longer Arnie held on to his confidence.

"She came here," he finally answered, shooting Roman a sideways glance. "Bitches just can't resist me," he added snidely, eyes returning to mine. "Cute little brunette, on a vintage Indian bike. She sweet-talked her way into a poker game by showing her tits, and then burned through a wad of bills getting us plastered. Guess that made it easier for her to corner Gordon in the can and fuck the information she wanted out of him."

One of his men snorted. "I thought she broke his fingers to get him to talk."

Arnie smirked. "I like my version better. I think Gordon does, too."

"And what information was she after, exactly?" My voice was smooth honey. Slow. I had to keep it together. At least until we had what we needed from him for the case. My personal vendetta could wait its turn.

Arnie licked the side of his mouth, slowly rolling his tongue along the underside of his top lip. "The same information you were *pumping* me for last summer."

"She wanted to know where the Scarlett Inn had moved?"

Roman asked.

Arnie nodded. "She wasn't very happy when she found out it was gone, along with any trace of Scarlett. Broke another one of Gordon's fingers just for spite."

"If she returns, give us a call, and we'll come take her off your hands," Roman said.

"Right. That's exactly what I'll do if the bitch finds her way back into my den." His sarcasm drew a chorus of snickers from his pack.

Roman holstered his firearm. "Let's go." He jerked his head, motioning for me to follow him to a crusty, steel door that looked like someone had tried to pry it open with a crowbar at one point or another.

If the bartender had called in reinforcements, slipping out the back was a safe move—even if a little gutless. That fear didn't seem to escape our hosts. Yellow ringed their pupils as they watched Roman retreat.

Arnie gave me a hungry look. "Come back and see me anytime, sweetheart."

I didn't move. My eyes were locked on his, and I couldn't even bring myself to blink. I didn't trust the fucker. I'd never give him my back.

He puckered his lips, blew me a kiss, and then turned around to head back to the table.

That's when I snatched him.

One hand grabbed the back of Arnie's jacket, and the other tangled in his greasy hair. He was bigger than me, but not by much. Still, I used his momentum to my advantage, pushing my weight into his back and riding him to the floor.

"Jenna!" Roman shouted. I hissed at him, my fangs extending at the same time. He jerked to a halt halfway between the back door and me.

"Not yet." A growl laced my voice. It hummed eagerly in my chest.

I was so tired of letting monsters that deserved to burn slip through my fingers. Roman was partially to blame for that. He'd stopped me from shooting Scarlett, and he'd allowed Arnie to walk free last summer.

It wasn't right. Arnie was just as guilty as his brother. He was a pathetic coward. He'd roll on anyone he could to get out of paying for his sins.

Not tonight.

I pressed my knee into his spine and pulled his head back until he groaned in protest.

"Call your bitch off, Roman! I told you everything! What else do you want?" he said through clenched teeth.

"Don't you remember? You owe me a good time, *sweetheart*." I yanked his hair back and sank my fangs into the tendon bulging along the side of his neck.

Arnie screamed. It was the sound of panic, pain,

and…*excitement*. It fueled me. I sucked sharply at his vein, not a hint of gentleness in my touch.

When I'd had a good, long drink of his heady blood, I spit him out, pushing his face into the floor where it made a wet noise against the concrete. None of his cronies moved to help. They were frozen to their chairs, watching with wide, wild eyes that weren't human anymore.

"Now we can go," I purred as I stepped over their heap of a boss. He remained sprawled and moaning on the floor.

Roman pushed the back door wide with one hand, holding it open for me as his eyes swept the room one last time, pausing on the faces we'd now have to watch out for.

Making enemies was delicate work.

Chapter Eleven

Roman gripped the steering wheel with both hands and hardly let off the gas as he turned onto the ramp to get back on I-55. Then he stomped on the accelerator again. The SUV roared, and the tires squealed as we merged into traffic.

"What the hell is wrong with you?" he finally asked, eyes zeroing in on some distant point ahead of us as if he were afraid to look at me.

"You warned him that I hadn't fed." I glanced out my window and rubbed a finger over my bottom lip where Arnie's blood was drying into a tacky film. My reflection cracked a smug grin.

"That's not how Blood Vice operates, Jenna." Roman changed lanes and cut around a line of cars as if worried someone might be following us. "Stooping to their level will only turn this into a supernatural gang war. That's why we stick to the book and make them play by our rules—"

"Our rules suck." I glared at him. "That asshole raped and turned who knows how many girls, and you think as long as he jumps when you say 'when,' that his crimes should be forgiven?" My chest heaved. I couldn't tell what I wanted to do more, scream or cry.

"It's not a perfect system." His tone softened with regret. "But it's the best one we have right now."

"I'm not sorry I bit him." I lifted my chin, unwavering in my self-righteousness. "He deserved it."

Roman sighed. "He deserves a lot more than that. I suppose we all do."

My cell phone vibrated in my pocket, bringing our tense exchange to a close. I was surprised to find Collins' number on the screen. I accepted the call and pressed the button for the speaker.

"You've got us both. Did you find her?"

"Maybe," Collins said. The click of a keyboard sounded in the background. "This person arrived on a motorcycle anyway."

"Vintage Indian?" Roman asked.

"How'd you guess?"

"Never mind that," I said. "Did you get a look at her plate?"

"Yup. Running it now." Collins cleared his throat. "Heather Anne Miller—wait, this can't be right."

"What?" I pressed, unable to suffer through even the briefest silence.

"DMV records say Miller was born in sixty-nine, but this girl on the tape barely looks drinking age."

"Plastic surgery?" I suggested.

"No surgeon is that good." Collins harrumphed. "My guess? Either the bike is borrowed or stolen, or—"

"She's more than just a donor," Roman finished with a frown. "She's half-sired."

"Is her address in the city?" I asked Collins.

"Jennings." The keyboard rattled in the background again. "It's an apartment. I'll text you the address."

"Thanks. We'll head that way." I hung up and glanced at Roman. He had an uncomfortable air about him. "Talk to me."

He was quiet for a minute longer. Then he took a deep breath, and his shoulders squared. "We're not just questioning this one. We have to bring her in."

"For breaking a few fingers?" I snorted. "You mean you're not willing to let her tattle her way out of hot water like you did Arnie?"

"Ursula doesn't have House Lilith's blessing to anoint another potential scion. Certainly not after abandoning her last two."

"What will happen to her?" I asked. He fell quiet again, letting my imagination fill in the gory details. "Roman?"

"At the very least, she'll be contained until Ursula's blood fully evacuates her system. The rest is up to the council."

"And how does the council usually handle these situations?" I turned to gaze out my window as we passed the Gateway Arch, lit up against the night sky. The heart of the city glowed around us and reflected off the Mississippi River just east of the highway.

"That all depends on the outcome of the trial against the vampire who did the anointing," Roman answered.

Collins' words about being viewed as an extension of me and having to pay for my crimes echoed in my mind. It was all kinds of wrong, but making a vampire's harem suffer was no doubt an effective punishment.

"She's only in her fifties," I said, grasping for a silver lining. "Losing her half-sired status shouldn't kill her."

Roman's brow furrowed. "Unless she suffers from some mortal disease."

My heart pinched with guilt. If Roman lost his half-sired status, he'd be dead within months. Maybe weeks. Our blood infidelity was a life-or-death gamble. We both knew it, but we were pretending that we didn't.

"You got that address?" Roman said, avoiding my stare. He fingered a button on the dash, bringing up the GPS settings.

Miller lived in an unremarkable apartment complex. A few kids bundled in coats and knit hats were playing ball in the back corner of the parking lot where a rickety hoop had been anchored to an electric pole. A streetlight a few yards above lit their makeshift court.

The building manager buzzed Roman and me in and happily handed over a key to Miller's apartment after seeing our badges. He seemed relieved to learn that we weren't there for him. His bloodshot eyes blinked nervously, and every sentence ended with *dude* or *man*, no matter which of us he addressed. When he opened the door to his own apartment and slipped back inside, I smelled pizza and weed.

Roman and I took the stairs up to the third floor. The hallway was empty. The sound of a television hummed through the door of the first apartment, but the next two we passed were quiet, the tenants either out or bedded down for the night.

I waited until we'd reached Miller's door before drawing my Glock. Roman drew his pistol, too. He flattened himself against the wall on the side nearest the doorknob, carefully slipping the key into the deadbolt. Then he nodded to me and eased the door open.

"Federal agents," Roman announced. His voice was even, only as loud as it needed to be without alarming the entire building.

We spilled out of the narrow entryway and into the kitchen and living room, clicking on lights as we went. There wasn't much to see. The place was as tidy and sparsely decorated as a two-star hotel. I imagined Miller considered someplace else home.

In the hallway that led to the apartment's two bedrooms, we split off, checking closets and under beds before meeting in the bathroom sandwiched in the middle. I yanked back the shower curtain, revealing mildewed tile and a mostly empty bottle of cheap shampoo.

Roman ran a hand through his hair, mussing it in his frustration. He stalked into the living room and yanked back the curtains, revealing a sliding glass door that opened onto a balcony. There were no stairs leading down, but he leaned over the railing, squinting into the alley below as if he suspected our mark could have survived a jump.

I went for the refrigerator. Perishables always yielded useful information. In the door, I found a carton of milk that was good for another week, and a two-liter bottle of soda that was half-empty but still fizzing with carbonation.

"She's been here recently," I said as Roman stopped in the doorway of the tiny kitchen. I holstered my Glock and peeked inside a to-go box with a longhorn stamped on the lid, finding the remnants of a steak dinner. The bottom of the box was still warm. "I bet she comes back tonight, too."

"What makes you say that?" Roman asked, shooting a nervous glance over his shoulder.

I opened the box wider for him to see. "Why save your leftovers if you're just going to let them rot in your fridge?"

He nodded and rubbed his jaw. "We should put a couple cars on the building, watch for her return." He flipped his phone open and blinked at the screen, holding it farther away before his fingers began to move.

"I thought being half-sired meant you got the all fancy vamp mojo," I said.

"It does."

"You seem to be having an awful lot of trouble with your eyesight lately."

A stack of mail propped between the microwave and wall caught my attention. I snatched it up and began thumbing through it. When Roman didn't say anything, I paused to look up at him.

His cheeks flushed, and his frosty eyes darted away from me. "It wears off over time. I'm due to be anointed tomorrow night." He turned his back to me and retreated to the living room to complete his call.

I breathed in through my nose, trying to calm the wrath eating its way through my insides. Roman being anointed was a good thing. It meant that he got to keep living. I had no right to be jealous. I should be grateful.

I thumbed through the mail a second time, and again, none of it registered. The third time through, I focused long enough to read Heather Miller's name and the return labels, most belonging to utility companies. One from a custom knife shop out of Colorado Springs caught my eye.

I held it up as Roman joined me in the kitchen again and began rummaging through drawers.

"Looks like we might have brought guns to a knife fight."

"Darn our luck," he said with a wry grin. His fingers looped through the handle of a cabinet, and a soft click tickled my ears.

Something instinctive exploded in my blood, and I was suddenly on the opposite side of the kitchen, shoving Roman away from the cabinet as it sprang open. His back hit the wall hard, knocking the air from his lungs with a surprised *oomph*.

The snap and hiss of the trap finished before his exclamation did.

I gasped and looked down at my chest. The tail end of a silver dart jutted from the wool lapel of my blazer. A glass syringe was nestled in the shaft. It was empty, the plunger likely depressed on impact. Whatever had been inside it was now inside me.

The entry wound burned with each breath I sucked in, the heat quickly spreading into my arm and neck. I felt it inching inward too, toward my heart.

"*No, no, no.*" Roman pushed away from the wall. Bits of sheetrock crumbled from a cracked indentation left by his shoulders. He caught me as my legs gave out, and we both nearly collapsed to the linoleum floor.

"Ow," I said, mostly at the ruined wall. Miller would definitely know we'd been here now.

"I'm sorry," Roman said, his eyebrows drawing together.

"For wh*aaa*—" My words dragged out and warped into a clipped scream as he yanked the dart out of my chest. "*Ow*," I said, louder this time and right in his face.

"We're not out of the woods yet." Roman tugged me toward the door, but my legs refused to work. I couldn't decide if it was from shock or if the silver was just working that fast. After a few steps, he lost his patience and slid his free arm under my knees.

My brain felt sluggish, jiggling around in my skull as Roman carried me down the stairs. His boots echoed in the stairwell, and his breath panted across my face. He was straining from exertion. I was no waifish damsel, but he'd thrown me around like a ragdoll in the past without even breaking a sweat.

The limitations and dangers of his half-sired status slipped to the back of my mind as the silver reached for my heart. I felt it coil around an artery like vines choking a tree trunk.

I was running out of time.

Undead Biology 101. A vampire can heal almost any injury given enough time and enough blood—provided the injury isn't decapitation or an explosion. Even an otherwise mortal wound to the heart can heal if addressed quickly, and the only thing capable of slowing that healing process to a fatal crawl is silver poisoning.

The seeping hole above my right breast would have been fixable even as a human, but if the silver reached my heart first, it would spread through the rest of my body and attack the healing enzymes working to patch me up. And if there was enough silver in my blood, it had the potential to trigger a true death.

The queen's mortal wound had needed an extra dose of those enzymes to combat the silver in her system or, as the ancient vamps who had yet to unravel the science of our species believed, *the blood of one's enemy*. Where was a vampy foe when I needed one? I would have gladly drained Scarlett.

I thought of the bloodstone Ben had given me in Spero Heights. How I'd scoffed at it. I slipped my hand into the pocket of my blazer and searched for the smooth rock, wrapping my fingers around it as if it were a lucky charm. I had no idea if it would actually help or not, but it couldn't hurt.

There were other, less effective methods to heal minor silver wounds. I suspected that Roman had one in mind as he dragged me from Miller's apartment and into the driver's seat of the SUV. The kids playing ball were gone now, but even so, the tinted windows kept anyone from seeing my growing fangs as I gasped for my next breath.

Roman tore off his suit jacket and threw it in the passenger seat. He pushed a button to open the hatch of the SUV and disappeared, quickly returning with the tackle box of a first-aid kit he kept in back. He climbed in next to me and closed the driver's side door behind him. Then he shoved back the console and laid me across his lap.

The memory of our first blood exchange made my pulse skip, and I felt the silver skim the edges of my heart.

"We need to extract as much of the silver as possible," he said, dumping the contents of the first-aid box onto the dashboard. He fumbled through the supplies until he found a snakebite kit.

My consciousness faded around the edges, sweat rising up on my skin despite the chill in the air. I felt Roman move my blazer and blouse aside before something pinched and sucked at my skin.

The silver burned just as much on the way out as it had on the way in. A shiver rocked my shoulders as my eyes flickered open. Roman's angelic face hovered above mine. He shoved up one sleeve and pressed the inside of his wrist to my mouth.

"Drink, now," he demanded.

"Don't I need vampire blood?" I asked, my voice raw with confusion.

Roman shook his head. "Not if we got enough of the silver out. Besides, I take a selenium supplement—it's part of my cancer treatment, and it counteracts heavy metal toxicity. My blood is the next best thing to a vampire's, and right now, it's all you've got. Drink."

I knew I shouldn't. Even through the feverish confusion eating at my brain, I resisted. Roman could rush us back to the office, and Collins, as mad as he was with me, would offer up his blood in an instant. It was only a twenty-minute drive. Ten if we lit up the dash flashers and blasted the siren. There was a chance we could make it in time.

Wasn't this how we'd gotten into this mess in the first place?

Roman pushed down harder until my fangs hooked on his flesh. Blood hit my tongue, and my vampling instincts kicked in. All logic escaped me.

This was only the third time I'd fed from him, but each tasting had revealed a new flavor. I was picking up subtle notes that I hadn't detected before, as if he were some high-end wine. It had to be his half-sired nature. His blood had been cultivated and ripened to perfection.

The familiar stirrings of lust roped around my insides as

the small trace of remaining silver in my veins diluted. Soon, I'd be begging Roman to satisfy another hunger.

The two went hand in hand where he was concerned. There was no settling for one or the other. I wanted them both and at the same time. What good was having cake if you couldn't eat it, too?

Something tickled the hole in my chest, and I pulled away from Roman's wrist with a groan.

"Is it working?" he whispered, gently pushing my blazer off my shoulder to examine the wound again. The blouse I wore beneath was soaked through with blood. Roman tugged the material down so we could watch a small bit of silver ooze up and out of the wound as it healed. It drew a hiss from me.

"Hold still," he said, and used the cuff of his shirt to wipe it away. A small, star-shaped mark remained behind. The veins nearest pulsed a gray-green color beneath my skin, slowly fading as Roman's blood coursed through me.

"I need you," I whispered, my voice shifting between the fleeting pain and a desire that rolled over me like thrashing ocean waves, shoving me under before I had a chance to catch my breath.

"Roman," I pleaded, pressing my face into his hand as he cupped my cheek.

"I'm here. I'm yours." His words were a prayer I wanted to answer—that I *needed* to answer. The urge to anoint him struck me. When I remembered that I couldn't, I closed my eyes, straining to keep my envy and grief from spilling out and spoiling what we'd begun.

Roman's fingers dragged softly across my skin, tracing my jaw and trailing down the center of my throat. He paused at the collar of my blouse, letting his touch slide back and forth, just under the material and around his masterful handiwork.

His mouth brushed against mine, and the tip of his tongue slipped past my lips. I moaned as he completed the kiss.

Static crackled through a speaker on the dash, and then Vanessa's commanding voice sliced through our bliss, parting us like the Red Sea.

"Bravo Victor HQ to 7-12," she said. "Do you copy?"

I recoiled from Roman and shoved to the opposite side of the cab, pressing my back up against the passenger door. She couldn't see us through the radio, or at least, I didn't think she could. Either way, I felt like a trapped animal in the SUV.

Roman grabbed the transceiver from the dash and sucked in a deep breath before pushing the call button. "This is 7-12."

"The detail units you requested are in place. Report back to HQ."

"On our way. Over." Roman gave me a soft frown as he returned the transceiver to its cradle on the dash. "Let's hope

Miller is apprehended before she makes it inside her apartment and discovers she had visitors."

I nodded and rubbed the heel of my palm over my mouth, trying to wipe away the evidence of our latest mishap. I would have an easier time of it than Roman.

As his hand pulled away from the dash, blood trickled from his wrist and splashed onto the stretch of leather between us. He swore and grabbed his forearm, stopping a small stream as it headed for the bend of his elbow and the crumpled sleeve of his white dress shirt.

"Shit." I reached for the first-aid supplies on the dashboard, my nervous hands scattering more than they grasped as I tried to find a bandage. "Shit, shit, shit."

"Jenna." Roman waited for me to look at him. "Take a breath. We can do this."

"Can we? God, what *are* we doing?" I panted as the severity of the situation slid home. Vanessa was going to kill me. She would fire me and then kill me. Or worse, she'd insist that I be coffin-locked.

I'd never had an office romance as a human. I'd never even been tempted to. How did people pull this shit off on such a regular basis? I was completely out of my depth.

"We can do this," Roman said again. His voice sounded tired, and bags hung under his eyes. He looked like a ghost. He'd given too much blood recently and hadn't taken care of himself well enough. A lot of that was my fault.

He nodded at a wad of napkins hanging over the edge of the dashboard. I handed them to him when what I really wanted to do was lick his arm clean.

So stupid. Terrible idea, I silently reprimanded myself. His blood erased all reason.

"This could still heal before we get back to the office," Roman said. He squinted at his wrist in the dim streetlight filtering in from the parking lot.

I finally took that breath he'd suggested and snatched up a roll of gauze.

"Let's hope so."

Chapter Twelve

As Roman and I made our way across the city, I wondered how much longer we could keep torturing ourselves like this. From the looks of him, not very.

He couldn't continue giving his blood to both Vanessa and me. Donors shouldn't be shared. For good reason. A line had to be drawn soon, or he wouldn't survive our tenuous affair, but the obvious solution felt too much like defeat.

After we'd found Ursula—*if* we found Ursula—I would ask Vanessa to go ahead and put in the transfer request she had threatened. It didn't matter where I landed, as long as there were a few hundred miles between Roman and me. If we didn't see each other day in and day out, maybe we'd manage to keep our hands and mouths and blood to ourselves.

I thought of Mandy and her relationship with Serena. They were already struggling to make the long-distance thing work with Serena going to school in Columbia. Mandy wouldn't want to leave St. Louis, but there was a slim chance I could convince her to move to Chicago or Memphis, where the next two closest field offices were located. Though, she wouldn't be thrilled about it, and I wouldn't be mad if she refused. This was my problem, not hers.

I didn't even consider Collins. There was no way I'd ask

him to move simply because I couldn't keep my fangs in my mouth around Roman, and I had a feeling Collins was on his way out of my life anyway. I didn't blame him. Getting away from me was the safe, sane thing to do.

I'd have to sell my mother's house. Affording the taxes and utilities and maintenance on top of living expenses in a new city would be too much to manage. I'd also have to make arrangements to interview new harem donors—whether Mandy decided to come with me or not. And then there was the matter of giving up my personal, off-the-record hunt for Scarlett.

That one would really smart. But Roman…

He was worth a hundred discarded vendettas.

I glanced across the front seat of the SUV again, taking in the ragged mess he'd become for my sake and affection. I wanted to beg him to bypass the office and drive us straight on through to Spero Heights. We could change our names and carve out a little place for ourselves in the Midnight District. I'd work in a cheese factory if it meant having him to myself every night.

Knowing how long and how hard he'd worked for his current status was the only thing keeping me from making the suggestion. He'd risked too much for me already.

It was true that there were plenty of unsanctioned, half-sired donors out in the world. Most of them escaped the scrutiny of Blood Vice by keeping their noses clean and their heads down. But that wasn't how things worked within the noble families.

If they wanted to keep a finger in the political pot, they had to play by the rules, which meant formally requesting permission to half-sire or turn a donor. The noble families also paid vampiric taxes and pledged a scion to Blood Vice every century as part of their blood tithe to House Lilith and the high council. In return, they were granted certain privileges and precedence.

If I tried to make off with Vanessa's potential scion, she'd hunt me down, and she'd do it with House Lilith's blessing and all of Blood Vice's resources to assist her. She'd go after my harem. Then she'd go after my sister.

A cold bitterness slithered into my heart.

I had to stop wanting something I couldn't have—something that would destroy the few people I cared about in the world. Requesting the transfer was my only hope of getting through this unscathed.

Roman's hand found mine and squeezed. "You're thinking too hard," he said softly, his thumb skimming my knuckles. "One of the detail units will pick up Miller. Then we'll interrogate her and find out where Ursula is. We could have her delivered to the duke by morning."

He thought I was worried about the case. I nodded, not

trusting my voice. The Spero Heights escape plan still lingered on the tip of my tongue, so I bit it.

This is only the lifeblood bond, I tried to convince myself. *This isn't love. This can't be love.*

But even if it were, it didn't matter. There was no get-out-of-jail-free card for lovers in the Blood Decree. We could be in love all we wanted.

That didn't mean I could call Roman mine.

It took everything I had to face Vanessa again. I trained my eyes on her desk, at the space between her hands. She stood in front of her chair, leaning forward with her palms down, dark fingernails clicking against the glossy wood.

Roman waited beside me, hands folded behind his back, same as mine. It was the expected, respectful stance for briefing a superior. Tonight, with his bandaged wrist tucked under the cuff of his jacket, it felt more like we were trying to cover up a crime. Which, we absolutely were. I wondered if Vanessa could tell the difference.

"The Moreau Pack is the third largest in St. Louis County and the seventh largest in the state," she said, eyes focused on me. For once, I was glad for it. "And you just took a bite out of their alpha's brother—*after* he cooperated and answered your questions." She inhaled deeply and licked her lips. "Do you understand what you've done? The can of worms you've opened?"

I choked down my pride and dignity. "I'm sorry."

"No, you're not." She laughed, but it was a hateful sound. "And if I were you, I probably wouldn't be sorry either. But I'm not you. I'm the one who gets to clean up your mess. I'm the one who has to kiss ass to a mangy wolf for the sake of keeping his pack in line."

I scowled at her. "His pack—his own brother—was helping Scarlett turn homeless teens into sex slaves. That doesn't sound very *in line* to me."

Vanessa's eyes turned black, silencing my outburst. "I'm *sick* of hearing about Scarlett. I've warned you, Skye."

I ground my teeth. I was sick of *thinking* about Scarlett. My recent peek into Roman's past only made me despise her more. I wondered if that history troubled Vanessa, too. Was that why she'd taken Roman off the baroness's case as soon as she made captain?

After a tense moment of silence, Vanessa's pupils shrank back to a more human size. "Preventing supernatural anarchy is one of our top priorities at Blood Vice. Instigating it is not on the agenda. It's the exact *opposite* of your job. You're a loose cannon, and you're lucky the duke is so convinced of your worth, or you'd be facing termination over that little stunt."

"We're closing in on Ursula," Roman offered, attempting to relieve the tension and remove some of the heat from me despite his condition.

"Only if this last-ditch lead pans out," Vanessa said.

It almost sounded as if she hoped it wouldn't, just so she'd have a justifiable reason to get rid of me. I knew she didn't want an unsolved case on her resume so soon after her promotion, but it was beginning to seem like the lesser of two evils.

I'd given her plenty of reasons to want me gone. I'd been obsessed with a case that wasn't mine. I'd been neglectful with the one that was. And I was, according to Collins, not well respected by the rest of the team.

To be fair, I hadn't made much of an effort to interact with any of them outside of my own unit. The overwhelming majority of Blood Vice agents were vampires. Dr. Delph had called that one. I wasn't particularly fond of my new kin.

I thought of Sonja Starling and the timid friendship we'd formed at the bat cave. I guessed they couldn't all be so sensible and humane. So many of the vampires that I'd met were either cold and detached or scathing vipers. A few fell somewhere in between. Like Vanessa.

Being around them felt like playing a game of bipolar hot potato. You never knew whether they'd play by the rules or go off course and hurl the potato at your face instead. Or sidestep and let it splat on the floor. They were house cat moody and jungle cat dangerous. And I was supposed to be one of them now.

"You look like shit," Vanessa said—to Roman rather than me, though I was the one who jumped at her words.

"I skipped sleep to search through security footage from Bleeders." Roman shrugged.

I sighed and nodded in confirmation. "Didn't you say that you were due for anointment soon?" I stifled my envy and aimed for a casual tone as I turned back to Vanessa. "Maybe you should do that sooner rather than later. You'll want him to bring his A-game when we pick up Miller. She's a pro."

Vanessa's pupils swelled again. She stood up straighter, pulling her hands away from the desk. "Are you trying to tell me how to manage my harem, vampling?"

Vampling. Clearly, I'd struck a nerve.

"No, ma'am."

I became very interested in the toes of my shoes as Vanessa circled her desk to stand in front of me. It was her favorite intimidation tactic. She didn't have to scream or get belligerent. She'd just invade my personal space and get very quiet. Deathly still.

In those silent moments, I could feel the way her power resonated from within. The way it reached out and tried to dominate me, tried to smother me into submission. She wanted to make sure that I knew she was better than me. That she deserved to be here, and I was just some fleeting pet project of the duke's.

The idea seemed to drive her crazy, as if she felt threatened by my swift climb up the ranks. I had to admit, I was a bit surprised by how quickly I'd ended up here, too.

I swallowed and dared a glance up at her, but she wasn't looking at me anymore.

"Why do I smell blood?" she asked Roman, blinking strangely at him.

He struggled to make eye contact with her. "We had a little problem at Miller's apartment. There was a silver trap set up in the—"

"Are you hurt?"

"No, I'm fine," he stammered. "Jenna pushed me out of the way. She took a silver dart to the chest—"

Vanessa's attention snapped back to me. Her gaze crawled over my black blazer. The dart had hardly left an indentation in the wool fibers. Nothing like the damage it had done to my blouse. I touched the spot over my breast, wondering if I should take the blazer off to show her.

"Silver?" she whispered, eyes going black again. "Your mutt is camping, and your human was here. How are you healed?"

If only I were a statue, my features hidden behind a mask of stone. I needed a convincing lie, but I needed it sooner than my wounded heart could manage. Panic tore through me, and my face said all Vanessa needed to know.

"I invoke the right to a blood duel," she said, a growl carving up her voice. "Now."

It was Roman who pushed *me* out of the line of fire this time. He put himself between Vanessa and me, shoving my back against the closed office door.

"I couldn't let her die," he shouted over Vanessa's outraged scream as she reached for me. "I used the snakebite kit. She hardly needed a sip after that—and she saved my life last year. I owed it to her."

"You owe her nothing!" Vanessa shrieked. "It's my blood that keeps you alive. It's my house that took you in when no one else would. You're pledged to *me!*"

She slapped him across the face. Hard. It rocked his head to one side and split the side of his mouth open. A thin line of his blood shot through the air. It grazed my cheek, drawing a gasp from my parted lips. My fangs began to extend, budding automatically at the promise of violence.

Vanessa's fury rerouted. Her liquid eyes blinked as I reached up to touch the blood on my face. A brave cocktail of emotions tangled up my insides. Cold rage and defiance bubbled over, and before I could rein it in, my finger glided across my cheek, collecting Roman's blood.

"You don't deserve him," I said, and then dipped my finger into my mouth, sucking it clean.

Chapter Thirteen

"Go! Get out of here," Roman cried. "Get out of the city—at least until I calm her down."

"Calm me down?" Vanessa laughed in his face. She tried to dodge around him, but he caught her wrist and twisted until he was between us again.

"Go! Please, go," he pleaded, regret seeping from his tired eyes.

It wasn't for lack of strength that Vanessa let him restrain her. She didn't want to hurt him, her potential scion. This was her exercising restraint, I realized. Which lit a fire under my ass.

I reached for the doorknob and paused to look back at Roman. "Come with me," I said, not caring that Vanessa was right there, listening to our exchange.

"In your dreams, you little bitch!" She jerked her arm, trying to shake Roman's grip. He grunted at her efforts. The sleeve of his jacket fell down his arm, revealing the bandage over his wrist.

"Go." His voice broke, and I heard everything he wanted to say but couldn't. It whispered through my blood. "Take your personal vehicle and turn off your cell phone, it can be traced."

I didn't wait to be told again. I slipped out of the office

and slammed the door behind me.

Collins was in the lobby, shrugging into his down jacket. He'd found Miller in the security footage, and with eyes on her apartment, there wasn't much else for him to do. He was supposed to have the night off anyway.

I grabbed his arm and dragged him through the front doors out to the parking lot, ignoring the curious glances from a pair of agents on their way inside.

"What are you doing?" Collins snapped once we'd reached the Bronco.

"Vanessa knows, and she's out for blood." I squeezed the sides of my head, wondering how much worse I'd made everything. What was wrong with me? Behaving like a…like a *vampire*.

Collins blew out a heavy breath and glanced back at the building. I shoved him toward his Toyota parked a space down from me.

"Grab Laz and get out of town for a day or two. Give me time to fix this."

"You're gonna fix this?" Collins' bitter laugh stabbed at my heart. It was the sound of a friendship dying. He gave me a pitying look. "Jenna, there's no fixing this. That's why I put in my notice with Vanessa earlier and explained that I was leaving your harem."

I gulped down the cold night air, unable to hide my

surprise. "Why didn't you talk to me first?"

"It doesn't matter now." He shook his head. "You should run. While you still have time. Go get Mandy and disappear."

Mandy. I didn't even know if she had cell service at her campsite—but I knew I couldn't call her on my own phone. Thinking of it, I pulled the device out of my pocket and powered it off as I unlocked the driver's door of the Bronco.

"Good luck," Collins said, pushing it closed behind me.

I rolled down the window as I turned my key in the ignition. "I'm so sorry, Collins. I wish things had turned out differently."

"Me, too." He tucked his hands into his pockets and gave me a sad smile as I pulled out of the parking lot and made my escape down South 22nd Street.

I had no idea where I was going.

I had no idea if Vanessa would give chase, or if she'd send someone after me, and I was too terrified to go back to my house. I considered Spero Heights…but the thought of returning there without Roman... Tears seared the corners of my eyes.

Was this why sireless vamplings were so often put out of their misery? Did they all fall into a life of crime as effortlessly as I had?

I worried for Roman, but he'd begged me to leave. He'd begged me to leave and refused to come with me. That rejection in itself felt as if it were burning a hole through my chest.

I'd told Collins I would fix this, and I desperately wanted to. There had to be a way. If not for me, then for Roman, and Mandy, and Laura. I feared for them all. I had to make this right.

Maybe I could convince the duke to spare me—or at least Roman and the others—if I managed to find Ursula. Maybe he could sweet talk Vanessa down from the blood duel. Or maybe that was all wishful thinking, but it was better than the nothing I had otherwise.

Miller was my only lead. There were at least two units watching her place. Going there was a bad idea. I needed another option, and fast.

I went through the list of people who had been in contact with her and what we'd learned from them. Ben Macaulay thought she was a saint. He trusted her enough to loan her his vehicle and paid her to do odd jobs for him whenever she happened to drop by. I wouldn't be getting anything more out of him, and I didn't have time to spare to make a three-hour drive for a dead end.

Arnie Moreau had had a very different experience with Miller. Violent as it had been, I admired her for walking into a den of hungry wolves and having the balls to extract the information she wanted.

She was smart. Ruthless. I had a silver scar on my chest if I needed any more proof of that.

The only other person I knew of who'd interacted in some way with Miller was Lydia…at Bleeders. I hadn't gotten much information out of her during my last visit, but that was only because we'd run out of time.

I wasn't welcome at Bleeders. I'd been warned not to return. Zane, the faux-fanged manager, would be waiting for me, and he would make sure I didn't slip past him again. Going back there was a bad idea.

But I was fresh out of good ones.

I parked a couple of blocks away from the club. After going through so much of their security footage, I had a pretty good idea how easily they could spot my vehicle if they were watching for it. This was my last chance, so I couldn't botch even the smallest detail.

I crawled into the back of the Bronco to dig around and see what I had to work with. Other than my service Glock and the Browning I kept in my ankle holster, there was my shotgun. I'd forgotten about it after shooting skeet with Collins—likely for the last time.

I pushed the heartache aside and tried to focus. My

firearms would have to stay behind. Bleeders had metal detectors. Mandy's backpack from our previous visit was stuffed up under the back seat. I dumped it out, deciding she'd have to forgive me, especially after all the times she'd pilfered through my bathroom drawers and closet.

Among the candy wrappers and crumpled trash mags, I found a cheap, dollar-store makeup palette and the fishnet top she'd worn last time. It smelled funky, but being left to dry in a backpack for a few days would do that.

I stripped out of my blazer, and my skin instantly rippled with goosebumps. I'd turned the engine off, and the Bronco was not good at retaining heat. I blew into my hands and rubbed them together before hurrying along with this terrible idea I'd committed myself to.

My bloody blouse was no good. I yanked it over my head and pulled on the fishnet top over my black bra. It was racy, but with Bleeders' *anything goes* dress code, it would work. It had to.

I opened Mandy's cheap makeup kit and smeared my eyelids with shimmery, black shadow. I used a dark, charcoal color on the undersides of my cheekbones, giving them a sharper look. Then I pulled the elastic out of my hair and moved my ponytail up high on the crown of my head.

The look had to be wild enough that I'd blend in with the extravagant mix of patrons, but not so outlandish as to draw unwanted attention from the eyes in the sky. I had a bad feeling that the security staff would be watching anyone who showed interest in Lydia, too.

Damn. This would be some magic trick if I managed to pull it off.

I finished fine-tuning my hair and makeup before tucking all of my firearms under the back seat for safekeeping. I left my badge and cellphone in my blazer and stuffed it out of sight, as well. Then I climbed out of the Bronco and slipped in behind a small crowd moving down the sidewalk. With their leather pants and spiked chokers, their destination was no mystery.

On the human police force, we'd all heard rumors of underground clubs and raves. The culprits often turned out to be cheapskate owners who wanted to evade taxes and the hassle of legally obtaining a liquor license—or drug dealers who wanted a place to draw in droves of buyers with the promise of privacy and the option of using out in the open.

Bleeders was a horse of a different color. They didn't serve alcohol or illegal drugs. From what I'd seen, they made bank on nothing more than door fees and seriously overpriced fruit juice. The few guests who caused trouble were taken care of in-house, and no police—human or vampire—were ever called in for assistance.

I caught a glimpse of the doorman as my party neared the

entrance. His unfamiliar face was a relief, and it gave me the confidence to continue putting one foot in front of the other.

The lot I'd tagged along with each requested a white wristband. I doubted they were part of a harem, but it was an easy way for timid humans to get their feet wet in the club without having vampires actually approach them to request a bite. The doorman didn't seem convinced either, until I requested a black bracelet. I gave him a sharp smile and briefly extended my fangs when he hesitated.

"Can I join my harem now?" I asked sweetly.

The humans had already moved inside the belly of the club, so they weren't there to spoil my cover with their surprise or denial. The doorman nodded and slapped the wristband on me before turning to the next guest in line.

I kept to the outskirts of the main floor, pausing every so often to dance up against any random stranger who happened to flash a grin my way. A straight line for the juice bar would be too obvious, too desperate. I needed to exercise patience tonight. I would have to take my sweet time tracking down Lydia.

The music lapsed for a split second, and then a new song started up. It boomed in my ears, the bass making the floor shudder as if a train were approaching, the electric squeal of a guitar playing the part of the conductor's whistle. A spinning strobe light overhead froze and then cut a slow sweep across the mirrored wall.

The effect made the crowd squeal with delight, and it was the perfect opportunity for me to steal a glance up at Lydia's usual perch.

She was here. There was a man with her—a human, from the red bracelet he wore. Lydia seemed uninterested in whatever he was saying, but she didn't blow him off. She wasn't making waves. Her yellow bracelet glowed under the black lights above the bar. It clashed with her red and black rockabilly dress, though the fifties look suited her.

My heart rattled in time with the music as it took off in a more dance-worthy direction, and I spun around as Lydia looked out at the crowd. I couldn't let her see me yet. She was far too likely to report me to a bouncer or slip out the back door to avoid the confrontation altogether.

My hip accidentally knocked into someone on the dance floor, and I offered a playful smile when they looked up. The man was wearing black jeans and a spike-studded vest over a white dress shirt. One foot on solid ground, and one tapping gently on the lid of a casket. Just my speed.

"Shake it, baby fangs," he shouted to be heard over the crowd.

The pet name was one Sonja had called me. I struggled to hold my smile in place, and then my eyes snagged on the man's red bracelet. I shimmied closer to him, lifting my chin over his shoulder.

"Are you thirsty?" I asked. His eyebrows shot up, and a flirty grin lit his face.

"The question is, are you?"

I linked my fingers with his and pulled him deeper into the club, in the direction of where Lydia waited. Maybe a little liquid courage would pacify me until I made it that far.

Drinking from strangers didn't sound as unbearably awkward as it had before my training at the bat cave, when I'd had a loaner harem of misfit blood dolls—one of which had been killed by an accomplice of Scarlett's. Another painful memory plucked at my heartstrings.

All the kind, fragile souls who befriended me in this new world seemed to eventually find themselves on the altar of my shortcomings. I was dangerous to be around.

You make *yourself dangerous to be around.*

Collins' accusation came back to slap me in the face. Here I was, proving him right. But what else could I do? Tuck tail and run? That wasn't my style, and it wouldn't keep Vanessa from coming down on the people I cared about in her quest for revenge.

No. There had to be a better way.

The man attached to my hand flagged a waitress and requested a mango and dragonfruit concoction while I selected a booth with a clear view of the bar. I handed the woman a twenty and told her to keep the change.

"Are you new to the area?" the man asked as I pulled the curtains closed, dimming the light show and cutting the music down to a more conversational volume.

"No," I answered truthfully. "I've been here once or twice before."

He sat on the bench that lined the inside of the booth and ran a hand over the leather upholstery. My eyes immediately went to the mirror above us, first checking for bouncers, and then taking note of Lydia's position.

"You sure?" the man said. "You seem extra fascinated with the place for a repeat visit."

"Just enjoying the show."

"It's something, huh?" He folded his hands in his lap. "What's your preference? Neck, or wrist?" *Jumping right to it then.* I liked this guy already. If I weren't so desperate to stay under the radar, I might've asked to interview him for my harem.

"Wrist. At least, for our first time."

He smiled at that. "You haven't even tasted me yet, and you're already making plans to turn me into a regular?"

"It's our first time either way." I shrugged. "Then we'll see who wants whom as a regular."

A slender arm parted the curtains just long enough to deposit a hurricane glass full of juice and floating fruit onto the table. Then it was gone, as if a ghost had delivered the beverage. The service at Bleeders was flawless. It made me wish I hadn't worn out my welcome so soon.

"How about heat level?" my one-night donor asked next.

"Excuse me?"

"Friendly touching only? First base? Let's get a room after?" he clarified.

"Uh…" I swallowed and thought of the room I'd shared with Roman. Then I tried to remember the platonic dynamic I'd had with my harem at the bat cave. "Let's go with friendly for now. First time and all."

First and only time, I silently added. I didn't need to scare him off with the cock-block just yet. Not until I had a strategy in place for Lydia.

The man shrugged as if it didn't matter to him one way or the other, though the corners of his smiled sagged slightly. He picked up the glass of juice I'd bought for him and took a long gulp from the rim, coming away from it with a cherry between his teeth.

"You're in for a treat," he said, slowly chewing the piece of fruit. "I'm vegan, and I haven't donated blood in three weeks."

I grinned and sat down beside him. "I'll have to buy you another juice before I leave."

I'd learned my lesson with Lydia and wouldn't be tipping

again. The taboo nature of exchanging blood for money had escaped me. Even Mandy had spoken with censure about the girls in Spero Heights charging for blood lattes at the bistro.

The man pushed back the sleeve of his dress shirt, revealing a handful of small puncture scars. They were smooth, hardly noticeable until they caught some fragment of light. I took his arm in both hands and rubbed my thumbs over the stretch of skin between his wrist and the bend of his elbow, massaging the veins.

He could play it as cool as he wanted. I could feel the giddy beat of his pulse.

Over the past two months, I'd grown used to drinking blood from a cup again. My misadventures with Roman had been fueled by passion and were none too gentle. It took me a moment to remember that delicate middle ground I'd shared with Natalie and her friends.

Just thinking her name probed some broken thing inside of me that I hadn't fully addressed since returning from Denver. For now, it was just one more death I blamed Scarlett for—just one more reason I wanted to make her suffer.

My new friend sucked in a nervous breath as my fingernails bit into his flesh. His dark, caramel-colored eyes widened, and I caught a glimpse of uncertainty in his stare. I wondered how long he'd had red-bracelet status.

"Sorry." I gave him a bashful smile and resumed

massaging. "New blood jitters."

"Right. Sure," he said, an uneasy laugh whispering in behind his words.

Once the tension in his shoulders released, and he didn't look so much like an alarmed cat about to bolt, I extended my fangs. His breath hitched again, but it was the good kind of anxious this time.

I closed my eyes and pictured Natalie before wrapping my mouth around the curve of his arm, letting the weight of my fangs do the work of breaking skin. The gentle touch drew a relieved sigh from his lips.

Warm blood trickled onto my tongue. I let it accumulate before swallowing, taking my time and resisting the urge to suck at his vein. I wasn't especially hungry. I'd had Arnie's and Roman's blood already tonight. Even with the silver injury that Roman had healed, I was satiated. More sated than I'd felt in some time.

This third meal was a bonus, and it went a long way to soothing my hopeless anxiety. That is until something jabbed the side of my neck and lit up my world with hot, electric misery.

My fangs ripped out of the man's arm, but I was in too much pain to manage a scream. My fingernails dragged over his skin, and he made a startled noise as he struggled to get away from me. I collapsed sideways onto the leather bench and rolled onto my back, blinking up at the lights dancing overhead.

"Well, if it isn't the little party trick." Zane, the wannabe vamp manager of the club, grinned at me from the booth's parted curtains. He held a stun gun in one hand. When he noticed me looking at it, he pressed the button, and the device lit up with a crackle of blue electricity.

"Well…" I rasped. "If it isn't Count Denturla."

He went for my stomach this time, pressing the business end of the stun gun to the strip of exposed flesh between the waistband of my pants and the hem of my see-through top. I gritted my teeth and groaned through the pain.

"What'd I tell you?" Zane said to one of the bouncers standing behind him. "A glutton for punishment. Let's take her upstairs. The boss is waiting."

Chapter Fourteen

The two bouncer flunkies following Zane's orders all but dragged me into an elevator tucked along the wall between the row of booths and the juice bar. We caught a few surprised looks, but no one tried to stop them or demanded to know what I'd done to deserve such treatment.

Zane stepped inside with us, shooting me a cocky grin before he gave me his back. I had half a mind to kick him in the ass, right through the gap in the doors as they slid shut. My feet hadn't been restrained. It would have been easy. Instead, I searched the bar outside, taking in the curious faces. I didn't see Lydia among them.

Once the elevator doors had closed, Zane swiped his arm in front of the control panel. The watch on his wrist beeped, and then we began to move. It was similar to the tech used at the bat cave. I wasn't sure why, but that put me on edge.

The elevator climbed slowly, giving the illusion that we were going up higher than we actually were. I'd assessed the building well enough to know there could only be one or two floors above the main level. The vaulted ceilings with their flashing lights and industrial ductwork were too high to allow for anything more than that.

The elevator doors opened into a dark lobby. On one side, a long row of glass windows revealed a room crammed with monitors. They were anchored to the walls and set along the length of a desk that stretched around the perimeter of the room. Red dots blinked in the corners of the screens, confirming that the scenes playing were live—various angles of the dance floor, parking lots, back alley, and more.

Half a dozen people moved around the room, watching the footage, searching for any signs of misconduct. I hadn't stood a chance.

It was the door opposite this room that Zane and his goons escorted me through. There were no windows to give me a preview of what or who waited inside. So I assumed the worst.

Maybe some big, foreboding Godfather-type. Perhaps I'd be sleeping with the fishes by morning, concrete blocks tied to my ankles. I wondered if the sun would relieve my suffering. Would I burn up if I were surrounded by water? Didn't light only penetrate so deep? Who on earth could I pester with all my vampire trivia?

I squinted in the bright light of the room we entered, waiting for my eyes to adjust. My blood vision hadn't flared up yet. I was holding it back, conserving my energy until it was needed most—until I had a half-baked escape plan worth wasting it on.

The place looked like a ritzy loft apartment. It featured a variety of restored antique furniture and gadgets, including a

1920s radio cabinet and a perfectly polished iron maiden. Maybe this guy was more medieval than mobster in his torture techniques. *Lucky me.*

Against the back wall, stairwells led up and down, likely to a bedroom and a kitchen. The main living area we stood in was enormous, with a high ceiling and no divide between multiple sitting areas. A baby grand piano rested in one corner, opposite the iron maiden. Between the two, a small section of hardwood remained unfurnished, as if it might be a dance floor. I could imagine parties taking place in here. It was a bachelor pad if I'd ever seen one.

A man appeared near the stairwells. He wore a silk smoking jacket that made him look like a young Hugh Hefner. My blood vision throbbed once, just long enough to confirm he was a vampire.

"Special Agent Jenna Skye." He had a faint accent, maybe Russian, and he didn't sound particularly thrilled to be making my acquaintance.

"Who wants to know?" I asked, earning another love bite from Zane's stun gun.

"That will be enough," the man said calmly, backing off his fraud of a scion. "I'll take it from here. I need your eyes on the floor."

Zane stiffened at the dismissal, but he didn't say anything as he bowed his head and backed out of the room, taking the two bouncers with him.

I was left standing alone in the middle of the loft, unarmed yet unrestrained. My eyes took in the room a second time, searching for something, anything that I might use as a weapon.

"You may call me Radu," the man said, slipping his hands into the pockets of his fancy jacket. "Please, forgive Zane. He must put on a show for the others. Your encore appearance is no good for our reputation. My scion stands to inherit my business, so he takes it quite personally."

"Your scion?" I asked. "He's awfully…*human* for that title. Don't you think?"

"Ah." He shook a finger at me. "Dante said you were good."

"Dante? The duke?" I folded my arms.

"Yes," Radu said. He crossed the room, heading for the piano where a crystal decanter service set rested on a tray atop the glossy, wooden lid. The dark liquid he poured into a glass was no doubt blood. He held it out to me. "Would you like?"

"No, thank you," I said.

Radu shrugged and put the crystal stopper back in the decanter. He took a sip from the glass before turning back to me. "The duke and I are old friends. This is why he keeps his soldiers out of my house, and I help him take care of…less savory business in our community."

"Look, I don't want to cause trouble." I let my arms drop to my sides. I didn't know if I believed this guy or not, but if he wanted to claim that he was pals with the duke, I was going to make him prove it. "I'm trying to locate someone—for the duke," I added with a pointed look.

"Yes. Dante has told me of your search for Ursula." Radu lifted an eyebrow. "So I am curious why you seem more interested in Scarlett. Isn't that whom you asked my fair Lydia about?"

"Uh…" I felt my face flush. Quite the busybody, wasn't he? "Ursula is looking for Scarlett, so my questions about her were relevant."

Radu nodded, but the look on his face said he didn't quite buy my line of reasoning. "Still, your captain should have put your request to question her at my club through the proper channels. My guests expect a certain measure of anonymity. We do not simply sell them a good time and a sip of blood, Agent Skye. They expect privacy and freedom from oppression and discrimination. Nosy federal agents do not promote the atmosphere we vow to provide."

"A formal request? Like the one Blood Vice put in for access to your security footage last summer?" I said, folding my arms again. "I was under the impression that you didn't play well with the authorities."

"Were you not granted access?" Radu laughed at my

surprise. "My dear, if I didn't want you to have access to my security footage, you wouldn't have gotten it. Do not misunderstand. Blood Vice's tech team is quite adept. Mine is just better."

"Then how…" I blinked, trying to figure out just what the hell I was missing here.

"My chief of security fields all network breaches and requests approval or denial from me. I allow them when I see fit. Sometimes, even when Blood Vice doesn't make a formal request," he added with a knowing grin.

"Does…does the captain of the St. Louis field office know about this?" I asked.

"Of course." He shrugged and took another sip of blood. "Though, she's not as gracious as the former captain. Our joint efforts are, for obvious reasons, off the record, but she is greedy with the credit where House Lilith is concerned. She didn't even thank me for the courtesy call last Sunday, when I spotted you and your lot in the club. And she failed to mention that you'd be here again tonight. I assume she is ignorant of this visit, as well?"

The question sounded like a threat from any angle. If he went ahead and called Vanessa now, I was screwed. But the only reason he'd have for not calling her would be so he could teach me a lesson himself. What had he called it? *Unsavory business?*

"Shall I call on her?" he asked, a teasing note in his voice. My anxiety wasn't lost on him. "Will Agent Knight in shining armor come for you again?" He paused as if waiting for me to fill in the blanks. When I didn't, he sighed. "Why do I get the feeling the right hand does not know what the left is doing?"

I snorted. "To Vanessa Sorano, I'm probably more like a failing appendix."

"Hmm." He nodded slowly. "Not a fan of yours either, I take it." He sat on the piano bench and folded his legs. "Truthfully, I'd rather not involve her. She's left a…bad taste in my mouth. But I also cannot allow you to terrorize my clientele. You understand?"

"I do." I pressed my lips together as I imagined those concrete blocks around my ankles again.

Radu swirled the blood in his glass and frowned at me. "Whatever shall we do to resolve this?"

I took a deep, slow breath. It was time to go all in. "Help me get the information I need from Lydia, and I'll personally see to it that the queen knows of your contribution in finding Ursula."

"And you'll stay clear of my club in the future?" he asked as if that were the most important part of this bargain we were striking.

"Yes, absolutely. I swear it." The breath in my lungs swelled hopefully as Radu tapped a finger against his chin, considering my offer.

"We'll have to be careful how we approach this," he said. "The severe reputation of Bleeders and House Vlad must remain intact."

House Vlad? As in, Vlad the Impaler? No way. I couldn't even bring myself to ask if there was a link. I'd lose my nerve and start searching for a means of fight or flight again. I needed that focus for the plan I was piecing together. This would be a long shot.

"We may need your reputation in order to pull this off," I said. I nodded at an antique rotary phone on a small table near the entrance. "Does that thing work?"

Radu grinned. "My dear, I'm a practical man. Everything in this room works."

My eyes briefly slid to the iron maiden before darting back to the phone. "May I?"

He opened his hand to the side. "Please." Then he stood and placed his empty glass back on the tray. "I suppose I should change. I never dirty my hands while wearing silk." He headed across the room, pausing at the mouth of the stairwell leading up. "If I find you're throwing vapors at me, dear, I'll be dirtying my hands with you tonight, as well."

I nodded, not quite sure how to respond to the threat. I didn't plan on throwing anything—except maybe a party after we'd captured Ursula and Vanessa swore off her blood duel.

I waited for Radu to disappear upstairs before making my call. The antique handset was delicate. I held it away from my face, afraid to soil its shiny surface with my makeup, and then fingered in Mandy's cell number from memory.

My heart throbbed in my throat with each ring. I hated that every element of this plan hinged on the one before it, like a set of dominos that required each piece to be perfectly aligned. When Mandy answered on the fourth ring, I nearly cried with relief.

"Mandy!" I gasped.

"Calm your tits," she grumbled, her voice heavy with sleep. "I have an alarm set for 4:00 A.M. I said I'd be back before sunrise, and I will be."

I chewed my bottom lip. "What if I need you sooner?"

"Where's Collins?"

My breath shuddered at the question. "He's no longer part of the harem, and he put in his notice with Blood Vice."

"What? Why? That asshole!"

"It's not his fault," I said. "Mandy, I screwed everything up. *Everything.* There's still time to fix it, but I need your help. It's bad."

She swore under her breath. "I'll get dressed and see who I can wake up for an earlier ride."

"Actually, I think I can bring this problem to you. In fact, that would probably be best." I dropped my voice to a whisper. "There's a *slight* chance there are agents looking for me in the city right now."

Mandy swore again. "I guess you really did screw the pooch this time."

"You have no idea." I sighed, trying to decide if I should go into my list of sins over a line that was likely bugged. How much did I want this Radu to know about my hazardous situation? How might it affect his agreement to help me?

"Why didn't your name come up on my caller ID?" Mandy asked.

"I'm at Bleeders."

"What the hell, Jenna? How many fires are you starting tonight?"

"It's okay. I'm safe here. I think," I said, glancing around the room to see if I was still alone. This night had certainly taken an unexpected turn. "You're at Meramac, right?"

"Yeah," Mandy said. I heard a zipper and pictured her stepping out of her tent, probably for more privacy. Werewolves had exceptional hearing, and she was camping with at least a dozen of them—who were all in law enforcement.

"Didn't you say something about an old motel around there?" I asked.

"That was only if a bad storm blew through. We managed at the campsite."

"Okay. Perfect. I'm going to need you to check into a room."

"Oookay?"

"Under the name Ruby Lillard," I added.

Mandy groaned. "Does this plan involve bad company?"

"The worst."

There was a floor beneath the one that held the observation room and swanky loft apartment. I rode the elevator down to it with Radu, my personal tour guide. He'd changed into a sharp, modern suit and had slicked back his hair with some product that made it gleam in the light. Very villain chic.

The new level was…eerie. We stepped out into a long hallway that stretched into darkness, an ominous illusion that made it appear as if it could go on forever. Our footsteps echoed off the concrete floor and walls. We passed a few closed doors and then a bloody handprint smeared across a section of wall. I pretended not to notice.

This was more what I'd expected after being dragged from the feeding booth. It reflected the barbaric reputation that patrons whispered about in the shadows. Radu might provide them with privacy and freedom from outside authority, but he did not take kindly to anyone who disrupted his carefully crafted playground.

It was hard not to imagine how differently my night could have gone if he'd had Zane deliver me here instead of to his loft. If he had known that I'd gone rogue…it could have been me on the opposite side of the glass window we stopped in front of, where Lydia sat sobbing hysterically.

She'd taken the bandana out of her hair and twisted it in her hands, touching it to her nose every so often. Her eyes swept wildly around the room, sliding right past us when they reached the window. It was two-way glass, I realized.

Zane approached us from the other side of the hallway. His eyes landed on me, and he scowled before giving his attention to Radu. "What now?" he asked.

The vampire retrieved an earpiece and a small, clip-on microphone from his pocket. He handed the earpiece to Zane and the mic to me. "You'll interrogate her, taking lead from Agent Skye."

Zane's eyes widened. His jaw flexed as he looked from me to his pretend sire. "Sir?"

"Is there a problem?" Radu asked. The calm control in his voice carried a darkness I was fairly certain I didn't want to see unleashed. I tried to keep a neutral face, doing my best not to provoke Zane any more than I already had.

"No problem, sir," he answered, slipping the earpiece in

place. He turned to me next, assuming a blank expression. "How would you like to begin?"

I glanced through the window, taking in Lydia's miserable condition. Her makeup smeared in all directions over her face, made only worse by her efforts with the bandana. She looked pissed and terrified all at the same time. Radu had been right about this being dirty work.

"Tell her that you know she's affiliated with Scarlett," I said.

Zane snorted. "She'll only deny it."

"That's when you'll sympathize and demand that she warn the baroness about what you found out when you *questioned* me."

Zane nodded, a hint of understanding lighting his eyes. "Okay. You'll pick up from there?" he asked, tapping his ear. I nodded.

"Take this with you." Radu pulled a bloodied handkerchief from another pocket. He'd come prepared. One side of his mouth drew up into a crooked grin when he caught my stare. "The anticipation of pain is almost sweeter than the act itself."

Zane accepted the cloth with an obedient nod. As he stepped into the room with Lydia, I clipped the mic onto the collar of my fishnet top. Standing next to Radu, I felt painfully underdressed. I couldn't wait to put my blazer back on.

Radu leaned closer to me, speaking into the mic from over my shoulder. "Knock if you can hear us, my scion."

Zane cleared his throat and rapped his knuckles on the corner of the table. It made Lydia jump as if she hadn't heard him enter over her sniffling sobs. He sat in the chair on the opposite side of the table and made a show of wiping his hands clean with the handkerchief.

"We know you're one of Scarlett's," he began.

"No!" Lydia blubbered, immediately denying it as Zane had predicted.

"That agent told us everything. Save your tears."

"I'm not! I swear!" Lydia pressed her fingers to her closed eyes. "I told her I didn't know anything."

"Ah, now we both know that's not true." Zane gave her a vicious smile, letting his fake fangs peek out. "You told her all about poor ol' Ricky. I heard it on the video with my own ears." Lydia gasped, but he waved his hand and went on. "I'm sure we can overlook that little betrayal—in exchange for your loyalty to our mutual friend, the baroness."

"B-but I don't…" Lydia hiccupped mid-sob. I could see the wheels turning behind her eyes. She was considering her words more carefully now. I'd believed her before when she denied any knowledge of Scarlett's whereabouts. But there was someone else I counted on her knowing.

Zane rested his elbows on the table and pretended to

clean his fingernails with Radu's horror-set hanky. "We asked that agent very nicely to tell us what she knew. Now, all we need you to do is call Scarlett and relay the information. That's it. Then you're free to go."

Lydia was on the verge of hyperventilating. *Free to go.* Those were the magic words.

"Okay." Her breath trembled hopefully. "Okay."

Zane cleared his throat, signaling me. I told him the name of the motel near Mandy's campsite and the name I'd asked her to register under.

"Tell her that the feds know," I said. "They're planning to pick her up after sunset tomorrow. She should warn Scarlett to leave now, before sunrise."

Radu gave me a sly grin. "You and I both know this poor girl has no ties to the baroness. Who do you expect her to feed this information to?"

"A scout of Ursula's," I said. His invaluable help deserved my honesty, but my answer seemed to trouble him.

"That's an awfully bold move for such a timid little blood doll." He frowned at Lydia through the glass window. "Are you sure she'll deliver?"

I'd given what she'd said about Scarlett a lot of thought.

The baroness fancies herself queen of the miscreants. She'll bite anyone who lets her—and plenty who don't. That doesn't make them harem material.

I knew that tone. Lydia was bitter. She'd been rejected, and I was betting the farm on her wanting to even the score. Blood Vice had let Scarlett get away so many times now, their investigation seemed like a bad joke. And Lydia had been caught in the crosshairs more than once.

But Annie… She was motivated by a half-sired bond to please her mistress. She would follow through where Blood Vice had failed. Lydia had to know that. There was also the fact that Lydia's exchange with Annie hadn't soiled her name. That had to count for something. Lydia's current predicament meant that she'd be too terrified to return to Bleeders anyway, so burning that bridge wouldn't matter.

It all made sense, but at the moment, it was still wishful thinking. So it took all the grit I could muster to look at Radu and say, "Yes. She'll deliver."

We turned back to the window and watched as Zane pushed a cell phone across the table and into Lydia's trembling hands. The sparkly bat charm dangling from the case told me it was likely hers, confiscated when she'd been brought in for questioning.

Her fingers moved swiftly over the screen, and I silently prayed it was Annie's number that she entered before pressing the phone to her ear and delivering the bait.

Chapter Fifteen

I half expected Radu to change his mind and not let me leave Bleeders. He just had that uncertain air about him. But we'd bonded over our joint effort to trick Lydia, and so he had Zane escort me out through a private exit into the back alley. It did *wonders* for my anxiety.

"I gotta tell you," Zane said as we walked past the spot where we'd exchanged heated words only a few days before. "I know we're supposed to be on the same side, but I really don't like you. If you're expecting an apology for the zapping, you can forget it."

I snorted. "I guess I'll be the bigger person then and apologize for mentioning your dental handicap in front of the help."

Zane groaned under his breath. "Do you know how much I paid for these? I thought they were perfect. How can you tell?"

We paused in the mouth of the alley, waiting for a car to pass. Zane stepped in behind a dumpster, staying out of sight. He couldn't be seen helping me escape—which is what any guest at Bleeders would assume if we were spotted together.

"Don't worry. Your secret is safe with me." I winked at him and then darted across the street.

Lydia's phone call had begun a countdown. I had to beat

Annie to the motel where Mandy waited. It was about an hour drive from the city. If I were lucky, I'd make it there by 11:00 P.M.

I activated the Eye of Blood on my way back to the Bronco, searching every shadow for signs of agents lying in wait. The world lit up in outlines and shades of red. When I realized I was in the clear, I took off at a full-on run. There wasn't a second to spare.

I had no idea where Annie was at the moment, but I assumed she would need to borrow a vehicle from someone in order to pick up Scarlett. Hopefully, that would buy me enough time to get into position.

Once in the Bronco, I fetched my blazer and yanked it on. Then I started the engine and cranked up the heat. The longer nights had their price. As I pulled out of the lot and made my way toward I-44, I wondered about the Blood Vice offices in Florida and Southern California. If I survived this mess I'd made, and if Mandy didn't want to transfer with me, maybe I'd consider those locations. There was still a slim chance I'd keep my job, right?

Or maybe I was just kidding myself with thinking I had a future at all. Only time would tell.

I tried to pacify myself with more unrealistic fantasies over the next hour, but it did little to calm the despair that had found a home in my heart since leaving Vanessa's office.

It didn't matter that Roman had begged me to leave. I still felt as if I had abandoned him to some awful fate. I wanted to believe that Vanessa wouldn't harm him. Not really. The slap she'd issued had been…intense. But she could have put him through a wall when he attempted to restrain her, and she didn't. Though, that probably would have been her next move, had he tried to leave with me.

I wanted to call and check on him, but it was too soon, and I wasn't a complete idiot. Odds were, Vanessa had someone in tech searching the grid for my phone at this very moment. As soon as it popped up, she'd be on her way.

If she had plans to outright kill me—which was safe to assume, considering the blood duel declaration—she'd come alone. It would be a short game of cat and mouse. Vanessa had been sired and trained by the best.

I'd given Mandy precise instructions, and I hoped like hell she remembered them all. I hadn't turned my phone back on yet, so she wouldn't be able to reach me if she had any questions or ran into any problems collecting the few things I'd requested of her.

At this hour, there were more truckers on the highway than anything else. I drove the speed limit, not wanting to risk a ticket, and eyeballed every driver that passed me, fearful that it might be Annie. I needed to get to the motel first. There was still prep work to be done.

By the time I exited the highway and began the slower trek down through the wooded area leading to the river, my nerves were raw hamburger. The moonless sky glittered with stars, but under the canopy of leafless limbs, darkness pooled around the Bronco. My headlights were the only sign of life for miles, the roar of the engine the only sound in the dead silence of winter.

I pressed down on the brake as the road curled into a steep decline, and then the motel appeared through the naked trees. It was nothing fancy. Just a series of small, brick buildings staggered across the hilly landscape. Numbered doors faced the parking lot, which was only partially lit by a floodlight over the sign for the office.

There weren't many guests—according to the three vehicles in the lot anyway. I couldn't be sure if Annie was familiar with me or my ride, but it wouldn't have surprised me. I stashed the Bronco down the road a ways, near the RV park along the river's edge. No one would pay much attention to it there, and it would be gone soon enough.

I strapped on my Glock and my mother's Browning—just in case everything went to hell in a hurry—before grabbing Mandy's makeup box and my cell phone. Then I locked up the Bronco and activated my blood vision long enough to make short work of the hike up through the trees.

Light glowed through the curtains of the last room of the

building farthest from the motel office. The rest of the windows were dark, either from the late hour or the abundant vacancy. There was practically zero guesswork. A silhouette of a girl in a dress appeared in front of the lit curtains, and my heart lurched.

Was it enough? Could this work? God, I needed this to work.

I hurried across the parking lot and tapped softly at the door. "It's me," I whispered, knowing Mandy's wolfy ears would hear me just fine.

The door opened, and a slender arm shot out, grabbing the front of my blazer. Mandy wrenched me inside the room and shut the door behind us, flipping the deadbolt as soon as she did. Then her arms were around my waist, squeezing the life out of me.

"Oh my God, Jenna. This is crazy. I can't believe we're doing this." She pressed her face into my shoulder and took a deep breath. "I'm so sorry I called your human life boring. And I'm sorry you don't like being a vampire. I wouldn't like being a bloodsucker either—"

"It's okay," I said, petting the curls in her hair. They looked just the way Scarlett's had at the barn. I grabbed Mandy's shoulders and held her away from me to get a look at the rest of her handiwork. "Is that the fanciest dress you could find?" I asked, touching a pink, ruffled sleeve.

Mandy's eyes widened with affront. "Dude, it's a weeknight in Podunk, 'Merica. I had to wolf it to the nearest 24-hour superstore, wearing my sweats like a fucking Christmas wreath around my neck. Then I had to trot my way back here with plastic sacks hanging from my mouth." She stuck her tongue out. "Is that fancy enough for you?"

"Sorry, sorry." I held up my hands. "I'm just nervous. You look great."

"Damn right, I do." She turned around and snatched a satiny, pink ribbon off the edge of the bed. "Now, let's put the bow on this gift horse."

I accepted the jab with pinched lips and traded her the ribbon for the makeup palette. We had plenty left to do and no idea how much time we were working with.

I secured the ribbon in her hair as she added blush to her cheeks. The finished result made my skin crawl. When I first encountered Scarlett, I'd thought she and Mandy could be sisters. Now, they could have passed for twins. As long as Annie wasn't long-lost pals with the baroness, she'd never tell the difference.

"Why Ruby Lillard?" Mandy asked as I dug through the rest of the supplies I'd had her pick up.

"It's one of Scarlett's aliases. All that detention time in the bat cave records room is finally paying off." I grabbed the roll of duct tape and fished my cell phone out of my pocket. "Skirt up, buttercup."

Mandy groaned. "I haven't shaved in four days. This is going to suck. I can already tell." She grabbed the ruffled hem of her dress and scrunched it up to her waist before propping her foot on the edge of the bed.

"We'll attach it to the inside of your thigh," I said, ripping off a long piece of tape. "The cotton shorts go on over, so it will stay hidden if your skirt flips up, and you should be able to power it on whether your hands are tied in the front or back."

"That's, um, awfully close to my…" Mandy wagged her eyebrows. "Make sure you have it on silent mode and not vibrate, mmkay?"

"Got it." I moved quickly, all the while stealing glances at the cheap alarm clock on the bedside table. Every little sound sent a bolt of adrenaline through my heart. My chest ached from the relentless panic I couldn't seem to stave off.

Mandy picked a wedgie and readjusted her skirt after pulling on the shorts. She wiggled her hips and made an uncomfortable face. "I sure hope you don't have one of those recalled models that's prone to overheating. My lady bits are hot enough."

"Where's your phone?" I asked, checking under the bags on the bedspread.

"Charging in the bathroom," Mandy said. "There's only

one outlet in here, and it's powering the lamp and a space heater. The desk lady said something about the propane tank getting low."

I headed to the back of the room where a door opened into a tiny space just big enough for a sink, toilet, and a half-sized tub and shower. I found Mandy's phone on top of the toilet tank, seeing as how the complimentary sliver of bar soap and a stiff, tightly rolled towel claimed the narrow ledge around the sink.

I tapped the screen and checked to make sure the battery was fully charged before unplugging it. Vanessa knew that Mandy would be camping somewhere around these parts. She might have asked tech to track my sole harem donor's mobile, too, but I doubted it would raise any alarms until we left the area. By then, Mandy would have powered on my cell, so it wouldn't matter.

Since my phone was the one with the biggest, reddest flag attached to it, I'd strapped it to Mandy's leg. No matter what happened to me, I needed Blood Vice to be there for Mandy—to keep her safe from Annie and, ultimately, from Ursula. That's where this wild bat chase was leading.

I needed Roman to be there for Mandy, too. In case Vanessa found me first. I knew he'd have a watchful friendly in the tech room. Or maybe he'd be in there himself. I held Mandy's phone against my chest, debating if I should turn it on and risk calling him. If everything went to shit—more so than it already had—I didn't want to regret not hearing his voice one last time.

"Jenna," Mandy hissed from the bedroom. "We have company."

"Shit." I flipped off the bathroom light and fumbled with the shower curtain. Annie was more resourceful than I'd expected. The original plan was to watch from the wooded lot across the road, but there was no leaving the room now. "Can you see what kind of vehicle it is?"

"I think it's one of those older Cadillacs. A real boat, you know? It's either gray or silver." Mandy gasped. "Oh my God. She's backing it in, right in front of the room. What do I do?"

"Keep the door locked and turn off the light," I said. "Make her work for it. If it's too easy, she'll get suspicious."

"Right. Right. Good idea."

I could hear the panic in her breath as she hurried across the room.

"You've got this, Mandy," I said, trying to encourage and calm her. She'd been through training at the bat cave, too— and a hell of a lot worse than that—but she was still only eighteen. I couldn't help but feel a pinch of guilt whenever I involved her in anything even remotely dangerous.

"Jenna?" she said, resolve steadying her voice. "Be careful."

"I will. You do the same."

Something smashed through the front window, and Mandy screamed. I bit my tongue and pressed my back against the shower wall. Glass crunched under someone's foot. Then something or someone thumped against the thin wall. Mandy made a strangled noise as the intruder shushed her.

It killed me to wait and do nothing. That it was part of the plan didn't make the feat any easier. The Glock dug into my hip, and I felt the weight of the Browning against my ankle. I could have stepped around the corner and ended this right now. God, I wanted to. But I had to think about the endgame.

Just a little longer, I pleaded with myself, hoping Mandy could hear the promise, too.

Glass crunched again, and then I heard a trunk lid close. A car door slammed a second later. The vehicle's engine revved as it sped off.

I counted to five, waiting to be sure there was enough distance between us that Miller wouldn't notice me leaving after her. Then I stumbled out of the shower stall and into the motel room. It was trashed. Glass littered the floor. The mattress lay skewed atop the box spring, and the small space heater had been knocked over.

"Jesus, Mary, and Joseph!" A spitfire of a little old lady appeared outside the broken window. Her wrinkled face bunched angrily as she took in the mess and me in the middle of it. "You're not the little missy I rented this room to," she said, shaking an arthritic finger at me. "I already called the *po-lice*. They're on their way."

She shrank away from me when I stepped through the window. There was a tall, possibly violent woman looming over her in the dead of night. Who could blame her?

I didn't flash my badge. There wasn't time for stories tonight, but I did spare her a curt nod before taking off down the hill toward the Bronco, Mandy's phone clutched in one hand. I pressed the power button and pulled up the GPS app that allowed us to track one another.

As soon as Mandy powered on my phone, I'd see exactly where she was. Until then, I could only assume Miller was taking her someplace near Spero Heights. Maybe Springfield. That's where I'd find Ursula, and the devil only knew who else. I hated to admit it, but I was going to need help.

Once I reached the Bronco, I punched in Roman's number and hit the call button.

Chapter Sixteen

"Mandy?"

"It's me," I said, steering the Bronco up a tight curve leading back to the highway.

"Jenna." My name on Roman's lips made anything sound possible. I took a breath as he continued. "You shouldn't have called. Vanessa may have a trace running on Mandy's phone, too."

"But you don't know for certain?" I'd take any shred of hope I could get my hands on. "It doesn't matter. My phone will show up on the grid soon enough, and I need you to convince Vanessa to send a team after it."

"She won't," Roman said. "Blood duels are too personal. Besides, she has all agents on standby for when Miller is captured. With the mood Vanessa's in, I don't doubt she'll extract Ursula's location by any means necessary."

I sniffed. "That might be a little difficult, considering Miller's not in the city and likely won't be returning tonight."

Roman was quiet a moment. "And…she has your phone?"

"No, Mandy does, but she's in the trunk of Miller's new ride. I have eyes on her taillights now." At least, I hoped those were the Cadillac's taillights up ahead. I couldn't risk getting any closer without alarming her.

"Dare I even ask how you pulled that off?" Roman laughed under his breath. He'd been soft-spoken the entire call.

"Are you…okay?" My heart flopped uselessly in my chest. As if there were anything I could do to help him if he weren't. So far, I'd only figured out how to make a bad situation worse.

"I've been ordered to wait in Vanessa's office," he confessed. "She's threatened to withhold my next anointment if I interfere with the blood duel."

"She can't do that—"

"Yes, she can." Roman sighed. "At least, by a day or two if she sees fit to discipline me. It is allowed by the rules of House Lilith." The strain in his voice ripped at my heart.

"Tell her…" This was hard, but it had to be done. I swallowed and tried again. "Tell her to call off the blood duel, help me bring in Ursula, and I'll ask the duke for a transfer myself."

"Jenna." He sounded doubtful, but we both knew it was the best offer we could make Vanessa. It was the *only* offer we could make her.

"Do it, Roman. Tell her I'll go to Alaska if you think it will make a difference," I said.

"I'll call you back." His tone shifted, and I suspected Vanessa had entered the room. He hung up without another word.

I dropped Mandy's phone on my lap and looked back up at the road, squinting through the trees for the distant taillights. The phone buzzed a second later. I stole a glance down at it, wondering if Roman was returning my call so soon, but it was the GPS app. Mandy had managed to turn on my phone.

About damn time.

She was almost a mile ahead of me. A few minutes later, Miller jumped onto I-44 West. I cringed, even though I'd expected it. We were moving farther away from Blood Vice. Even with flashers, sirens, and doubling the speed limit, backup would be a while.

Every minute that passed snowballed my doubt and dread. I could end up facing Ursula on my own. And I would, if for nothing more than to go down swinging to save Mandy. I couldn't ask her to help me set the trap and then just walk away.

I'd screwed up plenty over the past few days, but there was still a definite line that I'd refused to cross. Tossing Mandy to the wolves—or rather, tossing the wolf to the vampires—was miles beyond that line. Sireless vampling or not, I still had *some* integrity.

When Mandy's phone rang in my lap, I nearly drove off the road.

"Yes?" I answered without checking the caller ID.

"You really have a trace on Miller?" Vanessa asked by way of greeting. "This isn't just some ploy to compel me to call off the blood duel?" Her hatred echoed through the line, but she'd found her professional edge again since we'd parted ways—or rather, since I'd run for my life.

"Mandy is in the trunk of Miller's car," I said. "We convinced her that Mandy's Scarlett. Where do you think she'll take her?"

Vanessa breathed heavily into the phone. She was waiting for me to confirm the deal Roman had relayed before she extended any olive branches.

"We both want to solve this case." *Hopefully, more than we want to destroy each other*, I silently added. "I will beg the duke to be transferred when we're done. He'll be feeling extra appreciative, so it should be an easy yes."

"No bordering states," Vanessa said. She wouldn't make this easy. I knew there would be additional hoops to jump through.

"Deal."

"And you'll present me with a fresh harem donor as an official apology for your vampling debauchery."

That sounded like it had the potential to get awkward, but it was still better than dying in a blood duel. "Yes, ma'am."

"Good. I withdraw my challenge then."

I blew out a breath I hadn't realized I was holding. "Thank you."

"I have four units geared up and ready to head out," Vanessa said. "We'll meet you at Miller's destination."

"Okay."

"And Skye?" she said before I hung up. "Don't get trigger happy with the duchess. Wait for us."

"I will, as long as I can."

She ended the call without saying anything more.

My shoulders loosened a bit, and I rested easier against the driver's seat of the Bronco. I laughed to myself, giddy at the possibility that I might not die a true death tonight. It was just a tiny likelihood, but it was something to cling to.

My heart ached at the thought of Roman, but hopefully Vanessa would anoint him after our differences were settled tonight. I couldn't be distracted by the lacking future waiting beyond that.

Some part of me wanted to hope there was still a chance for Roman and I, however abstract it was at the moment. Maybe the solution would come to me later, once I'd accomplished the other impossible things on my list.

I checked the GPS app again to make sure I was still on Miller's trail yet a comfortable distance away. The shotgun in the back of the Bronco was only loaded with skeet shells. They weren't made of silver, but they'd still hurt, plenty.

I would keep my word and wait for Vanessa's assembled team as long as I could. But I wouldn't wait forever. I had more important promises to keep.

The farther Miller led me away from St. Louis, the more my anxiety returned, tightening my shoulders and creasing my brow. I needed this trip to last long enough for Blood Vice to catch up, but if it went on too long, arrangements would have to be made for the approaching day.

There were vamp-friendly bunkers scattered all over the country, but as an ignorant vampling, I didn't know where the vast majority were located. I didn't have friends or acquaintances in those communities. Hell, in the few circles I'd managed to briefly stumble into, I was pretty much considered a leper.

Despite the fact that I'd managed to form a lifeblood bond with my boss's half-sired donor, I didn't set out to make waves. I wasn't evil. I wasn't actively plotting to destroy anyone—well, *okay*, besides Scarlett. But did she really count? I didn't think so, especially now that I'd agreed to transfer out of state and those revenge plans had to be put on hold.

I'd thought Mandy would be eager to take Scarlett down, as well. But after we'd dismantled the Scarlett Inn, she'd seemed less enthusiastic about finding the baroness. Mandy had embraced her fate and was finding her place in the world. I had more than a decade on her, yet I refused to do the same.

Perhaps her therapy sessions with Dr. Delph had taught her how to let go of such ugly grudges. I wasn't sure I could. I'd compromise for now, for Roman's sake and my own. Alive was better than avenged. Anyway, Mandy seemed to think that Scarlett would lie low for a while now that Raphael was out of the picture. I had nothing but time. I could learn to be patient.

It was nearing 2:00 A.M. before the blinking dot on the map exited the highway. We were still maybe twenty minutes from Springfield. Miller turned south on a smaller state highway. Her speed dropped a fraction, and the traffic thinned, so I backed off, letting another quarter of a mile stretch between us.

Mandy's cell phone lit up in my lap. My eyes darted down, quickly reading the text on the screen.

20 MILES OUT. WAIT.

Vanessa was making good time, but maybe not good enough. Her message faded, and the map reappeared on the phone screen. The dot that represented Miller had made another turn.

This part of Missouri had a lot of farmland with thick stretches of woods in between. The houses were miles apart, perfect for avoiding nosy neighbors. Scarlett had put herself in the heart of a huge city, right in the mix of things. Ursula had been more careful. I supposed that was why Blood Vice hadn't found her even after twenty years of searching.

Miller's last turn was onto a long, private drive. Following beyond that point was a surefire way to blow the lid off this thing. So, I pulled onto the shoulder and killed the Bronco's engine.

I can be patient, I tried to convince myself. I gripped the steering wheel until it creaked under my fingers.

I can totally *be patient…if I'm a little closer to Mandy.*

The empty field between the highway and the house at the end of the drive didn't offer much cover, but with the Eye of Blood, I was sure I could find my way across it without being spotted. I wondered if Ursula had cameras around her little hideout. Did she have guards or a harem of ninjas? Had she half-sired anyone but Miller?

Half-sired humans were nothing to sneeze at. Even if Mandy hadn't planned to let Miller snatch her, and even with her wolfish strength, Ursula's potential scion would have given her a run for her money. Their strength increased with age, same as a vampire's. I had no doubt that Roman could take me in a fair fight. Of course, I was just a vampling.

I climbed out of the Bronco and circled to the back hatch where I collected my shotgun and stuffed a handful of target shells into the pocket of my blazer. The Glock and Browning were already strapped into their holsters. I wouldn't use them if I didn't have to.

I tucked Mandy's phone into my back pocket and locked up the Bronco before setting off across the field. The earth was hard under my dress shoes. If I'd known how much hell this night had in store for me, I would have gone with the special-ops gear. It would have been warmer, too.

I held the collar of my blazer tighter against my throat and tucked the shotgun under one arm. My hands were frozen. A light wind swept over the field, causing my ponytail to whip my face and my eyes to water. It was a mild night for winter, but the fishnet top under my jacket didn't do mild. It didn't do anything.

I rubbed a hand under my nose and blew hot breath into my fist, trying to thaw my fingers. When the ground evened out near the driveway, I picked up the pace. A few trees offered cover, but with the all-consuming darkness, I doubted I needed them.

The Cadillac was parked in a patch of gravel in front of the house. I ducked down behind it and pulled out Mandy's phone, checking the GPS app to see if she was still in the trunk. The blinking dot showed her somewhere inside the house. *Great.*

Kicking in the front door wasn't really an option if I

wanted to stay in Vanessa's good graces—or at least off her hit list. But sitting still wasn't going to cut it either. Adrenaline was eating me alive. I pushed away from the car and crept up to the house. There was bound to be a lit window somewhere.

The wraparound porch was empty. I stayed close to the lattice skirting that ran beneath it, stepping lightly so the gravel in the bordering flowerbeds didn't crunch. Where the porch ended, a hedgerow brushed up against the siding. It walled off a small patio behind the house, and that's where I found her.

I squatted behind the hedge and laid my shotgun over my knees, silently positioning myself until I found a suitable gap in the shrubbery. It wasn't much of a view, but with my blood vision, it was enough.

Ursula reclined in a lounge chair at the edge of the patio. Cheap solar lights glowed around her, staked into the frozen earth along the perimeter of the backyard. It butted up against empty fields on all sides. Rows of barren, tilled earth stretched on for miles, patiently waiting for spring.

Ursula looked like she was waiting, too. Her unblinking eyes stared up at the night sky, taking in the stars as if she wished they could swallow her whole. I'd seen pictures of her in the case file, but they were from the nineties. Vampires might not age in the traditional sense, but there was a maturity that showed in the way they carried themselves, and in the light of their eyes.

Ursula had aged. She was still beautiful, with deep red hair that lay in a thick braid over one shoulder. She wore an oversized cashmere sweater and a pair of leggings with riding boots. It was a casual, modern style that startled me. In the few portraits I'd seen of her with her sire, she'd been in frilly ball gowns. I realized now that she probably only rocked the regal look at the queen's parties. The reality was still a shocker.

The back door opened, and my heart jolted at the sound of Mandy's muffled protests. I ducked down farther behind the hedge, while at the same time trying to catch a glimpse of my girl.

Miller had put a bag over Mandy's head and silver cuffs around her wrists. I cringed, knowing how much those suckers burned. I'd have her out of them soon…as long as Vanessa hurried the hell up.

Ursula finally blinked. She twisted around in the lounge chair and put her boots down on the patio floor. A vein on her temple throbbed. "What…what is this?"

Miller smirked. "A late Christmas gift, my love." She pulled the bag off with all the flair of a magician, mussing the ribbon I'd tied in Mandy's curls.

Ursula's breath rushed out in a furious shudder. She stood and folded her hands over her chest as if stanching a wound. "Who is this girl? What is it you expect me to do with her?"

Miller blinked stiffly, her eyes searching Mandy's face and

her pink dress. "Isn't this…? I thought…" Her mouth opened and closed like a fish out of water. Something clicked, and her eyes zipped over the dark fields.

"What have you done?" Ursula whispered.

Miller took Mandy by the shoulders and turned her around. "Who are you?"

"Maybe you should have asked that before you snatched me out of my motel room," she said. Ever the smartass. Miller gave her a shake. Then she pulled a switchblade from the pocket of her leather jacket and put it to Mandy's throat. My hands tightened on the shotgun.

"Talk, or bleed. Those are your options," Miller hissed. She shoved Mandy down onto the lounge chair. The girl was unsettlingly quiet. She pressed her lips together as a wince tightened the skin around her eyes. Her wrists were raw and blistered under the silver cuffs.

"I just wanted to go camping," she grumbled. Her answer was as much for me as for Miller and Ursula. Guilt soured my stomach, and I vowed to take her camping myself after this case was closed.

"Annie?" Ursula's head turned, her ear tilting upward. "Do you hear that?"

Miller's breath fogged the air as she listened. I could hear it now, too. The distant hum of vehicles flying down the highway. On a road that didn't see that kind of action, it was curious. For someone who had been on the run for so long, it was a five-alarm omen.

"I'm so sorry." Miller gave Ursula a pained look. Tears sparkled in the corners of her eyes. "You have to run. I... I'll think of some way to stall them."

"Oh, Annie." Ursula's expression softened. She touched the other woman's chin and pressed a soft kiss to her forehead. "You've been more than I deserve."

"I'm so sorry," Miller repeated. She closed her eyes, and tears spilled down her cheeks.

"I know." Ursula's eyes slid to Mandy. "She does share a striking resemblance. Doesn't she? Perhaps I'll have a bite before departing."

Mandy's eyes lit with yellow fire, giving away her true nature. "Careful. I bite back."

"A wolf." Ursula circled the lounge chair, closing in on her. "Even better."

We were out of time. Vanessa and company were taking too long.

Mine, my blood hummed. I stood and took aim over the hedge with the shotgun.

"Quack, quack," I whispered.

Mandy rolled off the chair and flattened herself to the ground, and then I pulled the trigger.

Chapter Seventeen

Ursula's gasp ripped through the air. The blast had grazed her, pellets tearing at the sleeve of her sweater. She clutched her arm as blood spotted the gray cashmere. Cold, blue eyes narrowed at me.

"Run!" Miller shouted, putting herself between us. The shot had just missed her, but I had another ready to go.

"It's not silver," Ursula said, surprise hitching her voice.

"I was told I couldn't kill you, but no one said anything about not filling your face with buckshot." I kept the gun trained on the half-sired, ready to move the second the duchess did.

"Is this one yours?" Miller pointed the tip of her knife at Mandy, still flattened to the ground. She bent over and grabbed a handful of Mandy's hair, wrenching her to her feet before I had a chance to get off another shot.

"Never seen her before," I lied.

"Then you won't mind if I carve her up?" When I didn't reply, she sneered. "That's what I thought."

"You're surrounded." It was another lie, but I hoped it would be true soon enough. "Do yourself a favor and stand down."

"Go, Ursula," Miller said over her shoulder, putting the blade against Mandy's throat again. "I've got this."

The duchess made her escape into the back field. I wanted to go after her, but there was no way I'd leave Mandy to be sliced and diced. I ground my teeth and stepped around the hedgerow.

"Stay put," Miller demanded, the tip of her blade gouging Mandy's neck. Her eyes darted to Ursula's back, and mine followed, taking note of the direction she fled.

I activated the Eye of Blood and searched deeper into the distance. There was a nest of woods not far off. And beyond that, the interstate. From there, it was a short ride to Springfield. Then she'd disappear again, maybe for another twenty years. I couldn't let that happen.

I turned back to Miller, trying to think my way through the problem. Mandy tilted her chin in the air, pulling her throat away from the woman's blade as best she could while being yanked about by the hair. Her wild eyes sought mine. The look she gave me was one of annoyance. She was still playing the part. I returned her stare with a subtle nod.

Mandy twisted, letting the knife scrape across her skin as she slipped her cuffed hands inside Miller's hold. The woman pulled harder on her scalp, but it only helped turn Mandy in the direction she was already headed. She linked her cuffed hands and delivered a blow to the side of Miller's head, rocking her back a step.

Miller grunted at the impact, but managed to hang on to

Mandy's hair. The girl's eyes glowed brighter, and the bones in her face began to shift under her skin. It was a terrifying sight, no matter how many times I'd witnessed her do it. That glimpse of the beast beneath was enough to make my breath catch every time.

That fear reflected in Miller's face, too. She pulled her knife back, priming to deliver a killing blow. It was the window I needed.

The buckshot dotted Mandy's shoulder, but most of it found its way into Miller's outstretched arm. She screamed and released both Mandy and the knife.

Mandy took the opportunity to swing her linked hands at the woman again, this time delivering a batter's uppercut right under Miller's chin. When it was clear the woman was unconscious, Mandy knelt down and started picking through her pockets—I assumed looking for the keys to her cuffs.

"Are you good?" I asked, inching toward the field.

"Yeah," Mandy snapped. "Get out of here already. I didn't play dress-up for nothing."

I tore off. My blood vision painted the night red and the stars bright pink. It was almost too intense, the stark color with no lines to break it up, but I tried to focus on the braid slapping against Ursula's back ahead of me. She was nearing the trees.

One hand still gripped her wounded arm. Vanessa would

not be happy about that, but I had a feeling she'd be even less thrilled if Ursula got away.

A narrow path curled along the edge of the field. It was either a private drive or a country road. I couldn't be sure without checking the map. I tried to focus on the ground in front of me, jumping over the upturned earth. It was tiring and slowed my progress, but a twisted ankle wouldn't buy any extra time.

The cold air burned in my lungs, and the shotgun felt heavier with each step. The Eye of Blood was draining my energy. I could tell by the way it pulsed at the edges of my sight, but I pushed on, determined to chase Ursula to the ends of the Earth—or into the rising sun—if that's what it took.

This was one monster that would not get away from me.

Headlights sliced across the tree line, and then the beam centered on the road up ahead. Two SUVs barreled down the gravel, sending up a cloud of dust in their wake. Victory was on the horizon.

I paused to bend over and catch my breath, but I kept my eyes on Ursula. She'd seen the vehicles, too. The duchess stood in the empty field between us, looking back and forth as if trying to decide what to do next.

She stumbled and fell to her knees, chest heaving from her useless marathon. A look of defeat and despair shadowed her glossy eyes, and her sobs echoed across the field. They stabbed at my heart and made me question everything I thought I knew about her.

She's a monster. I had to hold on to that fact. Scarlett had been good at tricking sympathy out of others, too. I wouldn't make that mistake again. No matter how much my blood responded to Ursula's suffering.

She threw back her head and looked at the sky, her breath fogging upward like a smoke signal. I stalked in closer as the SUVs parked along the ditch, my eyes searching for familiar faces. When I spotted Roman, I loosed a trembling breath of relief.

He was here, and I wanted nothing more than to run into his arms. But then Vanessa appeared beside him. Roman cowered under her fierce, scolding gaze, and when she pointed him back to the SUV, he retreated without question. His eyes skimmed the field, landing briefly on me before he closed the passenger door behind him.

My fingers tightened around the shotgun as Vanessa and three more agents spread out and entered the field from the opposite side. They all wore tactical gear and carried the Moba M4 rifles we were trained with at the bat cave. I reached Ursula at the same time they did, completing the circle.

Vanessa gave me a critical scowl, and I remembered the makeup I'd put on for the trip to Bleeders. I glanced down and noticed that the fishnet top was peeking out above the collar of my blazer, too. *Super* professional.

One of the agents slipped the strap of their rifle over one shoulder and took Ursula's uninjured arm. They helped her up and escorted her to the SUV Roman waited in. Once she was secured, Vanessa turned her attention back to me.

Her green eyes glowed in the dark. My blood vision was gone, completely tapped out. Not even she could stir it to life right now.

I held my breath, wondering if Vanessa would go back on her word about the blood duel. Maybe she'd shoot me right here and now and leave my bleeding corpse in the field for the sun to find. It was only a few hours off.

"Starsgard and Miller have already been picked up," she finally said. "I've ordered another agent to retrieve your vehicle and drive it back to the city." My heart dropped, but then she added, "You'll ride with Erickson. We're to report to the duke straightaway."

The three agents in Erickson's SUV didn't say a word the entire way to the duke's manor in Ladue. They wouldn't even look at me. I didn't care. The peace and quiet was welcome, and I had too much on my mind to be bothered with their snobbery anyway.

I'd been relieved of all three of my guns before being escorted into the back seat. Vanessa wasn't fooling around. If I didn't request and receive the duke's approval for a transfer tonight, her withdrawal of the blood duel was null and void. This was her fixing the game—making sure she was perfectly poised to kill me the second I failed.

Now that I'd made it this far, I was actually considering the possibility that the duke wouldn't grant me a transfer. If that happened, I wasn't sure what I'd do. Maybe Vanessa would settle for me quitting Blood Vice and making the move out of state on my own.

My future was quickly progressing from grim to manic-depressive. I wished Mandy were in the SUV with me. I needed someone to talk to—and I was terrified what all of this would mean for her future, too.

It was pushing 6:00 A.M. when we finally pulled into Ladue. Half a dozen SUVs filed into the circular drive at the duke's manor. He and an alarming number of guards waited outside in the cold, eager to see Ursula with their own eyes I suspected.

Dante was wrapped in a long, wool coat. His gloved hands were folded in front of him, bright eyes shining hopefully. He seemed…cheerful. I wondered if the Vampiric High Council even knew that Ursula had been found. Wouldn't they expect the duchess to be properly detained before her trial?

Vanessa's SUV stopped in front of the duke's entourage. She jumped out and circled the vehicle, immediately opening the back door for Ursula to exit. Twenty years of waiting would not tolerate a second more. I climbed out of Erickson's SUV in time to witness the reunion, and I did my best to ignore the fact that two agents shadowed my every step.

Dante made an affronted noise when he saw the blood on Ursula's sweater. He embraced her tightly, disregarding her refusal to hug him back.

"You poor thing," he cooed. "I can't even imagine what you've been through."

"Can't you?" Ursula lifted her chin, eyes darting from face to face until she found mine. "Are these not your warriors? Do they not follow your command?"

"Forgive me, cousin," Dante said, that angelic sympathy of his softening the lines of his face. "I did not expect them to be so overzealous." He shot Vanessa a hard look that she, in turn, passed on to me.

Two agents from an SUV farther down the line approached with Miller held between them, her hands cuffed behind her back.

"Your Grace?" one of the agents said, drawing his attention.

"This is a personal donor of yours?" Dante pulled away

from Ursula and blinked at Miller as if she were familiar.

The dead stare Ursula gave Miller chilled me to the core. "I don't care what you do with this one, as long as I never have to see her face again." She turned back to Dante. "Tell me you have fresh blood in the cellar."

Miller's shoulders trembled as they caved in toward her chest. She sobbed quietly, tears spilling from unblinking eyes, but she said nothing as the two men holding her arms turned her around and headed back to the SUV.

Dante folded his hands and offered Ursula a small bow. "I'll have Belinda bring a selection of our finest donors to your room once you're settled in and Harold's had a look at that arm." He nodded at two of his guards, and they escorted the duchess inside.

Then the duke turned to Vanessa. "Your request for an audience will have to be quick. I have much left to do this night, and only an hour until sunrise."

She bowed deeply to him. "Thank you, Your Grace." When she rose, her eyes found me again.

One of the agents at my back nudged me forward. I had half a mind to turn around and deck him just on principle. Instead, I joined Vanessa as she opened the front passenger door of her SUV and ordered Roman out. The three of us followed the duke inside and to his office.

My pulse thundered in my ears. The words I'd practiced

in my mind on the way here muddled, and all I could seem to focus on was Roman's vacant expression and the way he refused to look at me. This close, I could feel him in my blood. I could taste the lie that he was trying to swallow. It bruised my heart.

"Now," the duke said, stripping off his leather gloves and dropping them to his desk. "What is it that I can do for you and yours, Captain Sorano?"

Vanessa straightened. "I would like to file a grievance against Special Agent Jenna Skye. She has violated the Blood Decree by drinking from my pledged scion, Special Agent Roman Knight, without my consent."

"What?" I cried. "You agreed that you'd forgive me if I requested a transfer."

Vanessa narrowed her eyes at me. "I never said anything about forgiving you. I said I'd annul the blood duel. Filing a grievance is completely different."

"But…but all of that bargaining about no bordering states and offering you a fresh harem donor as an official apology," I said and clenched my hands into fists.

"It got you here, didn't it?" She gave me a smug grin, but it didn't reach her eyes.

I huffed and looked at Roman. "Did you know about this?"

"Even if he did, he's not required to tell you," Vanessa

snapped. "He's mine. Not yours. Not *ever*."

"Enough." The duke's quiet order held the authority of a man who had long ago established his place at the top of the food chain. The threat in his calm, detached voice sent a tremor through my shoulders.

Vanessa shrank away from him, bowing her head in submission. "Your Grace," she conceded with a shallow breath.

I dipped my head in an obligatory nod, but I kept my mouth shut. Every muscle in my body tensed. My lungs labored as I tried to steady my wrathful panting.

The duke folded his hands behind his back and walked a circle around the three of us, a hard, thoughtful look worrying his youthful face. I resisted the urge to twist my head around and follow him with my eyes. It would be more than rude—it would be an open admission of my lack of trust and respect for him. Those were things good little vamplings were expected to keep in check.

"All of this over a single blood doll?" He sighed and paused somewhere behind us. He wasn't breathing over our shoulders, but he didn't have to. Goosebumps tightened my skin as his tone softened. Coming from anyone else, it would have been disarming. It just made the duke seem that much more unpredictable.

"This complicates my plans," he said, mild

disappointment tingeing his words as if he were simply complaining about the weather. "But, fortunately, I can offer a solution."

Roman's sharp intake of breath jerked my attention to him as the duke took hold of his head, his thumbs hooking behind Roman's ears and fingers finding purchase on his temples and cheekbones.

"Wait! What are you—" I choked on the words as the duke wrenched Roman's head to one side.

Something cracked in Roman's neck, and he was suddenly facing me at an awkward angle, his icy eyes full of alarm. They blinked twice more, and then he was gone.

Chapter Eighteen

My world imploded in slow motion.

Dante released Roman's head, and he fell for what seemed like forever. My legs gave out, and I slid to the floor at the same time as Roman's body hit the hardwood.

"What have you done?" I said, cupping Roman's cheek. He looked so…young and innocent. Without the decades of worry he carried around in his conscious hours, the age when his mortality had been staunched by vampiric intervention was obvious.

Vanessa's breath trembled murderously. She hadn't moved, but she watched me touch Roman, her green eyes bleeding into black orbs when I pulled his head into my lap.

Dante retreated behind his desk and sighed. "I am not a therapist. My position is not for granting advice that you may take or leave. If you bring your troubles to my doorstep, you will accept the solutions I offer."

"Yes, Your Grace," Vanessa said. Her voice was rough with restrained emotion.

Dante picked up the phone on his desk. "Send in two of Sorano's agents," he said. When he hung up, he shrugged out of his coat and laid it on the corner of his desk. "Thank you for your service to the St. Louis field office, Vanessa. As of tonight, you are relieved of your captain position within Blood

Vice. You and your new vampling will be transferred back to Denver, to the Blood Authority Training Center. It should prove a more stable environment for nurturing a prized scion, don't you think?"

Vanessa's jaw flexed, but she averted her disappointed gaze to the floor. "Yes, Your Grace."

Someone knocked on the office door.

"Come in," Dante called out. The agents he'd requested entered, their eyes instantly falling on Roman's crumpled corpse.

He wasn't gone—not really—but I was too shocked to consider everything this meant for us. His blood was dead to me now. I would never experience it the way I had before. I would never have the opportunity to anoint him as my own.

Six hours. That's how long Sonja had said a heart needed to stop pumping before vampire blood fully took root. Roman would rise tonight as one of the undead. It was what he'd wanted—at least, it was what he'd wanted before our lifeblood bond.

"Please," Dante said to the agents. He waved his hand at Roman. "Help Agent Sorano retrieve her scion and get him home safely."

They nudged me aside and each took one of Roman's arms, hauling him upright. His head lolled to one side, chin bouncing against his chest. It would be healed before tonight, but it was still upsetting to watch.

Vanessa followed them out of the duke's office, and one of the house guards closed the door behind them. I remained alone on the floor, feeling the weight of the night crushing down on me.

"That is not a very dignified way to present yourself, Agent Skye," the duke said, taking a seat behind his desk. He wasn't done with me.

Of course he wasn't. I'd been a very bad vampling.

My limbs shook as I followed the subtle command and pulled myself off the floor. I swallowed and folded my hands behind my back. My tired eyes focused on the duke's face. The sympathetic lilt I'd noticed in his expression when we first met was still there, but it was less convincing.

He took a deep breath through his nose and sighed before resting his elbows on the desk and lacing his fingers together.

"This is not your fault," he said. "I expected too much of you. You are but a vampling."

The gentle tone of his voice irritated me. It was patronizing, as if he'd just settled a disagreement between two children fighting over a toy. I couldn't bring myself to respond, but I lowered my gaze for fear he would see the hatred churning inside me.

"I have staked my reputation on you, Agent Skye," he continued. "I promised the queen that I would look after you until she appoints your adoptive sire at Midsummer, and that's what I intend to do."

It sounded more like a threat than a promise. I stood perfectly still, waiting for him to deliver my fate. I had neither the energy nor the time to attempt to flee. The sun was on its way. I felt it tug at my bones, hanging on me every bit as miserably as my grief and defeat.

Dante picked up the phone on his desk again. "Send in three of my wolves and Agent Starsgard."

My heart shot into my throat. "She's done nothing wrong," I said as soon as he hung up. "Please, don't punish her for my mistake. I'll do anything you ask of me. I swear."

"Quiet." The command was calm, delivered with that ominous air of authority he possessed. It froze me in place. I was a rabbit in the snow, ears perked at the soft sounds of an approaching fox.

A moment later, Mandy and the three guards entered the office. Mandy was still wearing the pink dress, but she'd taken the ribbon out of her hair. She frowned at me, eyes wide with caution as she stopped in front of the duke's desk and folded her hands behind her back.

"You are Agent Skye's sole donor?" he asked.

Mandy dipped her head in a respectful nod. "Yes, Your Grace."

"You will decide now if you wish to remain a permanent

servant of her harem or sever ties before we proceed," he said.

Mandy blinked at me, worry bunching her eyebrows. She didn't want to leave, but she knew the shit was about to hit the fan. If she didn't get out while she had the chance, she'd be dragged down with me. I couldn't do that to her.

"This problem is mine." My voice choked, and I was forced to whisper. "You deserve to live the life you want."

Her hand shot out and grabbed mine. "I only have this life because of you. It's yours as much as it's mine, and I'm not going anywhere."

"It's settled then," the duke said, clapping his hands together. He turned to the three guards. "Take Agent Starsgard to the residence she and Agent Skye share and help her collect their personal effects. Then, return here."

Mandy gave my hand a squeeze before leaving with the guards. As werewolves, none of them had to fear the quickly approaching sunrise. Still, the immediacy of the request alarmed me—as had the fact that he hadn't waited another night so I could collect my things myself.

"You'll be staying here until Midsummer," he said. "I'll fill the role of your adoptive sire until you are given one officially, and as such, my first task will be to expunge your lingering human presence."

"Excuse me?" I wasn't sure I understood what he meant, but it didn't sound good.

"Your dwelling in University City will suffer an electrical fire, and a set of unidentifiable remains will be found to verify your official death record. It will relieve your pending sire of the task."

I huffed out an affronted noise. "I grew up in that house. I've lived there my entire life."

"And now that life is over," the duke said, lifting his eyebrows as if surprised by my resistance. He wasn't used to having his authority challenged. "You will remain here at the manor for the next five months and not leave without an escort of my choosing. Do you understand?" The frightening warning returned to his tone.

I bowed my head. "Yes, Your Grace."

Belinda, the duke's assistant, retrieved me from his office. She led me to a bedroom on the main floor, all the while explaining how things worked at the manor. I tried to listen to her, but my thoughts kept skipping back and forth between Roman's new condition and the idea of my childhood home being burned to the ground. What a shit show this day had become.

"Your personal donor will be given the room next to yours," Belinda said. "You'll also have access to the household harem. Their quarters are upstairs." She paused to pull the curtains away from the wall of windows at the back of the bedroom and rapped her knuckles on the thick glass. "This is double-paned and UV filtering. There's a steel shutter system as well, but it only activates if the glass is compromised." She folded her hands in front of her stomach and smiled at me.

"Okay," I said, unable to summon the gratitude she clearly expected.

The room was nice. It was more than nice. A white fur throw lay across the foot of the bed over a smooth, gray duvet. Above the bed hung a large, framed photograph of the rising sun, blazing against a pink and violet sky. The reminder that the night was almost over soothed me. I wanted it to be over. All of it.

"Your wolf will not return with your personal effects before daybreak," Belinda said. "But there are dressing robes and sleepwear in the en-suite closet if you desire."

"Okay," I said again, my voice fading to a whisper as I went to the windows. There was a sliding glass door hidden beneath the fold of the curtains. Beyond it stretched a terrace and then twilight, glowing through the thick bows of evergreens that bordered the property.

"Would you like me to send someone from the household harem to help you change and offer refreshment?" Belinda asked. She was trying so hard to be accommodating. The duke had told her to make sure my every need was met, but what I needed no longer existed.

"No. I can dress myself," I said. "And I'm not hungry."

"Is there…anything else I can do for you before sunrise?"

I turned and forced a small smile at her. "I'm fine. Thank you."

The magic words seemed to do the trick. Belinda bowed her head.

"Rest in peace, Agent Skye."

After she'd left, I slipped into the bathroom and stripped out of my clothes, discarding them in a hamper. I placed my badge, keys, and Mandy's cell phone on the counter. Then I found a white, silk robe in the closet and pulled it on before washing the makeup off my face at the sink.

I checked the top drawer of the vanity and found a full set of toiletries. The handles of the mirror, brush, and comb were imprinted with an ivy design that reminded me of the family tree I'd discovered in an ancient book in the bat cave library.

I picked up the comb and pulled the elastic out of my hair before raking through my tangles. Everything felt surreal, as if someone else were driving my body and going through the mindless minutiae. I couldn't do this for the next five months. It would drive me mad.

I glanced at Mandy's phone. The battery flashed that it was almost dead.

I considered calling Laura or Collins to let them know what was going on, but I just couldn't bring myself to deal with either of them right now. Then I thought of Alicia and Serena, and of how much they'd already been through because of me. I pressed my hands over my face and breathed through an onslaught of hot tears.

No. I couldn't do this for five months.

I couldn't do it for one more night.

I left the bathroom and made my way to the sliding glass door.

Chapter Nineteen

Sunrise was thirty minutes off. I leaned against the railing of the terrace and squinted at the sky as it took on more light. It tore at my eyes, adding to the flood of tears I couldn't seem to stop now that they'd begun.

Everything had gone to hell. I was ready to follow it there. Of the few people I cared about who would be allowed to know I hadn't actually died in a house fire, only Mandy and Roman mattered. But Roman would be in Denver soon, and I didn't think Mandy really understood what she'd signed up for. She would be better off without me.

This was for the best. I was tired of looking over my shoulder, of longing for things I could never have. I was tired of hurting.

"Not celebrating your victory, vampling?"

I jumped at the sound of Ursula's tight voice and wiped my face with the back of one hand as I faced her. She'd exited a door farther down, and I realized she'd been given a room next to mine that shared the outdoor space.

"I just want to be alone." I sniffled and rubbed the sleeve of my robe under my nose.

"Funny. That's all I wanted, too."

Ursula gave me a dark look as she approached, crossing the terrace with a slow, purposeful stride. She'd changed out of her bloodied clothes. White, silk pajama pants covered her legs, and a white camisole hung from her thin shoulders.

The arm I'd shot was wrapped with a bandage down to the bend of her elbow. When she noticed me looking at it, she smirked and tilted a small wine glass to her lips, sipping delicately at the dark blood inside. Questions lit up my mind, and I decided I had nothing to lose by putting them to her.

"Miller risked her life for you," I said. "Why would you just throw her away like that?"

Ursula's eyes widened, and she choked on her blood cocktail. A drop fell to the collar of her white top, quickly spreading into a dark stain. She pulled the glass away from her mouth and coughed into her hand before replying.

"You shot Annie. Why would you care what I do with her?"

I shrugged. "I'm just trying to understand how you could go from caring so deeply for someone to feeling nothing. How do you turn that off?"

"Annie was just a random blood bag," Ursula said, her eyes darting away from mine to take in the twilight creeping over the trees. "There are a few billion more just like her."

"Then why anoint her?" I asked.

"You think you know it all, do you?"

"If I did, I wouldn't be asking."

"Little orphan Annie." Ursula laughed bitterly. "She

wasn't always mine. She was meant to replace me, but after…" She sighed and took another careful sip of blood from her glass. "Annie needed me, and at the time, I needed her, too. Now that I've been dragged, kicking and screaming, back into this circus of a family, it's not safe for her to remain with me." There was longing in her voice, a yearning so deep that I felt compelled to apologize.

"I was only doing my job," I said. "The duke ordered me to find you, so I did."

Ursula sniffed. Her mouth stretched into a sharp, unfriendly smile. "Do you know what Annie's job was, vampling?"

"She was a scout, searching for your lost scions."

"Yes." She lifted an eyebrow. "And she was quite good. Your name passed her lips even before you were turned." The hairs on my arms rose as she crept closer. "A contact in Denver mentioned that you were sired by the late, great Pablo Zajalvo. Annie had another theory."

"What's that?" I asked.

She stopped directly in front of me. I could smell the blood on her breath. Her porcelain skin was flushed from the cold, but she remained unmoved by it, while I shivered uncontrollably, my bones aching and rattling. Whether I had January or Ursula to blame more for that was up for debate.

"Your arrival came about the same time my naughty

scions disappeared from St. Louis," she said, tilting her head to one side. Her glossy doe eyes blinked at me, long lashes sweeping her angular cheekbones. "There were rumors that they might have sired a bastard or two. Their discarded harem made quite the fuss in their quest to exterminate imposters they felt had stolen their imagined birthright and caused their masters to flee the city."

My breath felt thick in my throat. "There are a lot of rumors regarding your scions, but I wasn't assigned to their case."

"Not with Blood Vice anyway." Ursula rubbed the rim of her glass along her bottom lip. There were so many emotions wrapped up in her delicate features.

I didn't know what to say. She'd been trying to corral and tame her wayward scions, and I'd used that maternal aspiration against her. She also didn't seem to suspect that Raphael was dead. Her scrutiny made my heart want to boil in its own blood.

"Ursula," Dante called from the open door of her bedroom. "Come inside, darling. The sun draws near." He held out his hand, beckoning her.

Her curious eyes fell on me once more. "Until dusk, vampling."

I watched her leave and slip past the duke, tucking her shoulders in as he reached for her. The way she rebuffed his care seemed to distress him, but he offered me a gentle smile as he stepped out onto the terrace and closed the door behind him.

"You should be inside, too." He took in my white robe with a satisfied look, but his expression stalled when his eyes reached my face. "Come," he said, opening his arm toward the door to my room. "I've had blood delivered to your quarters."

I glanced at the sky lightening beyond the trees. It wouldn't be long now. I just needed a little more time.

"Jenna." My name was a warning on the duke's lips. "A dozen wolves are stationed around the perimeter of my estate. There is nowhere else to go."

I closed my eyes and leaned against the railing of the terrace, shuddering as the light grew more intense through my eyelids. A shadow fell over me, and then the duke's iron grasp was around my wrist. He dragged me to the doorway and ushered me inside, completely unaffected by my resistance.

"I have no scion," he said, closing the door behind us while keeping his grip on me. "So I do not pretend to be an expert at housebreaking one. But, understand, I will fulfill my promise to the queen by any means necessary." He backed me across the room and pushed me onto the bed, finally releasing my wrist.

The impulse to spill my darkest secrets to him was strong.

If I told him who my true sire was, maybe he'd let me roast in the sun like I'd planned. Or maybe he'd take me to the Vampiric High Council and have them coffin-lock me. Or maybe he'd torture Mandy since she'd sealed her fate by agreeing to be a permanent part of my harem.

"You've ruined everything," I said, settling on my current hell instead.

The duke gave me a withering look as he picked up a phone from the bedside table and dialed zero. "Lock the exterior doors of our new guests' rooms," he said to whoever answered. "Yes, all three for the time being."

I wondered if he suspected Ursula had similar plans to mine. She'd been less resistant, but perhaps she'd just been biding her time. She was as miserably trapped here as I was.

Dante hung up the phone and circled the bed. A tray holding a dainty teapot and two espresso cups rested on the opposite table from the phone. He filled one and held it out to me.

"Drink." When I didn't move to accept it, he added, "I will call in guards to force-feed you if necessary."

I swallowed and took the drink from him. He waited until I brought it to my lips before pouring a cup for himself. It was warm—much warmer than I'd expected—almost as if it had been heated to resemble the coffee we were pretending it was.

"I have a full schedule tonight," he said, pausing to sip at his cup of blood. "But Belinda will assign a guard to keep an eye on you."

"Of course she will." I cringed and finished off my blood in one swallow before placing the cup back on the tray. I was ready to be rid of him. Dawn couldn't come soon enough.

"I hope your attitude is much improved when next we meet." His eyes curiously drank me in as if he couldn't believe anyone would have the nerve to disrespect him—the Duke of House Lilith. He set his unfinished cup on the tray beside mine. "I'd hate to be forced to resort to unpleasant methods in order to compel your cooperation."

I was reminded that there were worse things than death and bowed my head. "Yes, Your Grace."

He hummed to himself and nodded, accepting my strained obedience for now. "We will speak again soon. Rest well."

He left quickly. A moment later, the sun grazed the horizon. My eyes closed, and I was gone before my head hit the pillow.

Chapter Twenty

I dreamt of Roman and Spero Heights again. It seemed like a million years had passed, but it had only been a couple of days. For a minute there, I'd really thought we had a fighting chance. How had everything gone so wrong so fast?

In the dream, Roman comforted me like he had at the hotel where we'd consummated our affair, breaking skin for the joy of it rather than out of necessity, and needlessly fueling the lifeblood bond that had captivated us both.

We have forever sprawled out before us. We don't need to have all the answers today.

From within the warm cocoon of his embrace, I would have believed anything he said. The memory soothed and ached at the same time.

There was forever, but there was no *us* it catered to, and certainly no answers waiting to fix what could never be undone. When the sun set, he would rise as a Sorano. Then, he would drink from someone the way I'd drunk from him. The thought destroyed me.

There was no comfort to be found in that reality.

I woke Thursday night to find Mandy curled against my side. She was in her favorite Metallica shirt and her angry unicorn pajama pants. It made me smile despite the hollow sadness aching in my chest. I tried to extract myself from the bed without waking her, but she jolted awake the second I moved.

"Did you really try to burn yourself up in the sun?" she whispered, tears creeping into her eyes before I had a chance to offer an explanation. "Because that's a super asshole thing to do after I agreed to stay here with you."

I sighed and dropped my head back to the pillow. "I'm not really thinking straight. A lot has happened."

"You're telling me." She sat upright and pulled her knees to her chest. "I was given two plastic tubs and told to pack only the things we couldn't live without. They're torching the house tonight, so you'd better go through your stuff and make sure I didn't miss anything."

The tubs were stacked near the door. I crawled off the bed and went to them, thinking about all the things that I knew I wouldn't find inside. I grabbed the top box and set it on the floor, kneeling down beside it. My fingers trembled over the lid as I tried to work up the courage to open it.

Mandy folded her arms over her knees. "I shot Laura a text so she won't freak out when she gets the call early tomorrow morning. She's an actress, so she should be able to pull off the mourning sister act. Is there anyone else you'd like to reach out to?"

I shook my head. "The duke probably wouldn't even

approve of Laura knowing. Let's leave it at her for now."

Mandy cleared her throat, and I could tell she was fighting back tears again. "I don't know how to tell Serena. This is going to shatter her. I'm supposed to help her mom move to Columbia next weekend, and now I don't even know if I'll be allowed to. This whole situation is so fucked up."

"Yeah." There was nothing to argue about there. I took a deep breath and opened the first tub.

The velvet box containing my mother's badge rested on top of a stack of clothes—my favorite jeans and the dress I'd worn to the All Hallows' Eve ball. The fire hydrant lamp from my bedside table was wrapped in a couple of tee shirts, and a few of my Mark Twain books were tucked in between my mother's scented candles and the framed picture of her and Maggie that I'd kept on the living room wall. I held it to my chest and sighed.

"I left the answering machine behind, but I grabbed the cassette out of it," Mandy said.

"Thank you. You're the best." I choked back a sob. "I'm so sorry I got us into this mess. I don't know how yet, but I swear, I'm going to make this right."

Her eyes dropped to the bedspread as if she didn't believe me. There was a disappointed sadness there that I couldn't ignore, but it was deserved. "They put the Bronco in the garage," she said, directing the conversation back to reality.

"They're going to torch it, too."

At least I still had the keys with the foam shark Maggie had mangled and the ceramic badge I'd made my mother in grade school. But other than those bittersweet mementos, and the few things in these boxes, I would have nothing to my name after tonight. My life insurance would pay out to Laura, and my checking and savings accounts were payable to her upon my death also.

I'd meant to change the POD to Mandy, but even with the extended winter daylight hours, getting into the bank before they closed was almost impossible. The task had been pushed farther and farther down my to-do list. I hadn't considered it a priority, seeing as how I planned to live forever.

"You had a few thousand dollars in the safe, too," Mandy said. "But the assholes who were sent with me took it. They said they'd turn it over to the duke for safekeeping. They let me pack your range Glock and the .380 you kept in the breadbox, but they made me empty the bullets out of them."

"Fair enough." I put the picture frame of Mom and Maggie back into the box and dug out a pair of jeans and a sweater before closing the lid. Even if we were supposed to be here for five months, this would never be home. I wasn't about to unpack my things. Not here.

"What are we going to do, Jenna?" Mandy hugged her

legs and stared out the windows. Dusk was fading quickly.

"You didn't understand what was going on when you agreed to this," I said. "I'll talk to the duke. Maybe he'll reconsider—"

Mandy's head snapped up, and she glared at me. "I could have shifted and bailed at the house if that's what I wanted to do, but it's not."

"Sorry." I propped my elbows on the plastic tub and rubbed my eyes with both hands. "I don't know what we're going to do. The queen is supposed to announce my new sire in five months. Until then, the duke is determined to fill the role."

"So what?" Mandy shrugged. "We're under house arrest until then? Are we fired from Blood Vice?"

My eyes watered, and I shook my head. "I don't know. I don't know anything anymore."

Mandy sucked in her bottom lip and dropped her legs off the side of the bed. Her brows knit together as she struggled to look at me. "I saw Roman this morning—when they carried him out. He was… Is he gonna be…?"

I sniffled and blinked back a tear. Something stirred in my chest—a panic and sadness and hunger that weren't wholly mine. "He's a vampire now. He and Vanessa will be in Denver before sunrise."

She nodded slowly. "I'd thought maybe someone told the

captain about him feeding you last summer after you jumped off that roof and tried to wrestle Scarlett's pet wolves out of a moving vehicle…but then someone mentioned a bite not healing, like it was a recent fuck-up."

My face warmed, and I looked away from her. I couldn't bring myself to go through the painful details again.

"I heard you took a bite out of Arnie Moreau, too." She sounded less broken up about that one.

"He looked at me the wrong way." I hitched a defiant eyebrow. "I'm not even a little sorry about that." She whispered out an amused laugh, but then her face turned serious again.

"You need more donors. Things like that don't happen if you're feeding regularly."

"I'll have access to the household harem while I'm here." I stood and put the plastic tub on top of the one I hadn't checked yet.

Mandy knew me well. I didn't doubt she'd saved the things that meant the most to me. She'd even been considerate when choosing the clothing. The sweater I hugged to my chest was the one Laura had gifted me for Christmas.

"I should take a shower," I said. If nothing else, it would help wash the sleep from my eyes and the gritty salt from my skin. Yesterday stuck to me like a bad habit.

I licked the corner of my chapped lips and tasted traces of stale blood from my three meals. Despite the excess, I swayed on my feet.

"Sit down," Mandy demanded, pointing at the bed as she hopped up. "You need blood first. I think I saw a cup in the bathroom."

She disappeared into the en-suite, and I reclined back against the pillows, waiting for the room to stop spinning. Even with as hard as I'd pushed myself yesterday, this was unusual.

Roman.

He was up now. I could feel him stirring in my blood. His death hadn't severed that bond, but from what I'd learned at the bat cave, it was supposed to speed the process along. For now, I was still bound to him.

A flood of his emotions spilled over to me, and I struggled just to breathe through the disorder and confusion. I wanted to go to him, but it was Vanessa who had claimed that right long ago. Where the hell was she? Why wasn't she fixing this agony?

A proper sire would have a donor prepared for their scion's first feeding. His turn had been unexpected, so maybe she was rushing to pull things together at the last minute. Or maybe she was punishing him for his insubordination and her resulting demotion.

My cell phone buzzed, vibrating against the surface of the bedside table. A scrap of duct tape lay across the battery cover. I blinked at it, wondering how much trouble Mandy had had with the removal. Then it buzzed again, and I realized it was ringing.

"Roman?" His name whispered past my lips as I answered the call.

"Are you safe?" he asked in a guarded voice.

"I'm at the duke's manor. He's keeping me here until Midsummer. Are *you* safe?"

"I am." His breath was even, but it sure seemed like he was struggling to keep it that way.

I slipped off the bed and stood by the window, watching the night finish blotting out the sky.

"Are you…sure?" I asked again.

"I'm just calling to say goodbye before we leave for Denver."

"You haven't fed yet," I said, as if that were a good enough reason to stall his exodus.

"How do you…?" He cleared his throat. "I don't have much time. You won't hear from me again, and you shouldn't try to call. I won't have cell service at the bat cave."

"So that's it? This is just…over?" I held my breath, longing to hear his on the other end of the line.

"This is how things are meant to be, Jenna."

"You don't believe that."

"We both know it's true," he said. "I can feel the lifeblood bond releasing already."

"Liar." My breath rushed out with a sob. I pressed a hand over my mouth to muffle it. A long pause stretched.

"I'm so sorry." Roman's voice was barely a whisper. I wondered if Vanessa were hovering nearby, urging him to hurry along his mutilation of my heart.

"If you feel nothing, then why do *I* still feel like I'm dying?" I demanded.

"I don't know."

"You don't know?" My voice trembled with the question.

"We have forever sprawled out before us. We don't need to have all the answers today."

"Roman…please…"

"Goodbye, Jenna."

The line clicked dead before I could say anything else. I stood at the window with the phone pressed painfully to my ear, trying my damnedest to reverse time. That seemed infinitely more useful than the Eye of Blood right now.

I picked apart every mistake I'd made, wishing like hell I could take them back. But I knew I'd do it all again. I couldn't even say that I'd be more careful or less likely to get caught. If anything, I would have been recklessly passionate and caved to Roman immediately after my return from Denver.

If I'd known how little time we would have before it was all ripped away, I wouldn't have wasted a single second of it on doubt or guilt. I might have even suggested running away, even knowing that he'd refuse. Even knowing how much this would hurt in the end.

I wanted to tell him all that and more. But none of it mattered now.

Roman was gone. Dead. The version of him that had been mine no longer existed. I blamed myself as much as I blamed Vanessa.

But above all, I blamed Dante Lilosa.

How stupid I'd been to think he was any different than the rest of his kin—*our* kin. The murderous heathens. Scarlett, Raphael, Ursula, Kassandra—I somehow doubted the queen's and prince's hands were any cleaner.

Last fall, I'd craved a vampire family to call my own. Now, I wanted to watch House Lilith burn. I wanted to light the match. Scarlett was still out there, and I'd find her eventually. For now, I had a new mark in mind.

If you can't beat them, join them…and destroy them from the inside.

House Lilith was doing a fair job of that on their own. Maybe one more murderous heathen in the mix could speed things along.

Catch up with Jenna and company in…

THICKER THAN BLOOD

BLOOD VICE BOOK FIVE

Available Now!

With her home and heart in ruins, Jenna is none too keen on the idea of helping the Duke of House Lilith—the man she holds responsible for everything wrong in her life. But when the Vampiric High Council summons Ursula, Duchess of House Lilith and Jenna's unsuspecting grandsire, to a trial where she's to stand accused of murdering her sire and abandoning her depraved scions, the duke is eager to strike a deal. If Jenna helps him protect Ursula, he will keep her darkest secret and put in a good word with the adoptive sire the queen assigns to her. Oh, and return her guns—provided she doesn't use them on him.

ACKNOWLEDGMENTS

I did a silly thing this past year and decided to write 4 books. Not gonna lie, there were days when I thought I'd shot myself in the foot with this goal. But…I pulled it off. Finishing Blood Dolls was a proud, exhausting achievement for me. And I muscled through it with a heavy heart.

My Uncle Joe, one of my favorite people in the world, was diagnosed with cancer in October of 2017, and we lost him just one month later. While helping clean out his apartment, I found a first edition of my very first novel on his book shelf—next to a book on world religions. He encouraged and inspired me in a lot of ways growing up, and he meant a great deal to so many people. The world is a sadder place without him.

These books don't happen without lots of help. So, as always, I owe thanks to the following awesome people: my husband, Paul, for doing his best to answer all my obscure firearm questions (*Would skeet target shells blow off someone's arm?*) and for being my sounding board, proofreader, muse, and so much more; my kiddo, Xavier, who made frequent trips into my writing cave to offer kisses and to share his snacks with me; my critique group, the Four Horsemen of the Bookocalypse: Kory M. Shrum, Monica La Porta, and Kathrine Pendleton; my sister, Justina Dodson, for being my lovely cover model; Rebecca Frank, for designing another amazing cover; Chelle Olson for whipping my words into shape (all remaining errors are my own); Hollie Jackson, for lending her musical voice to Jenna in the audiobooks; THE Professor George Shelley, for his invaluable literary advice and friendship; and all my Grim Readers online, for cheering me on and leaving reviews.

Thank you all so much! You guys are the best! ♥

ABOUT THE AUTHOR

USA Today bestselling fantasy author **Angela Roquet** is a great big weirdo. She lives in Missouri with her husband and son in a house stuffed with books, toys, skulls, owls, and glitter-speckled craft supplies. She's a member of SFWA and HWA, as well as the Four Horsemen of the Bookocalypse, her epic book critique group, where she's known as Death. When not swearing at the keyboard, she enjoys boating with her family at Lake of the Ozarks and reading books that raise eyebrows. You can find Angela online at
www.angelaroquet.com

If you enjoyed this book, please leave a review.
Your support and feedback are greatly appreciated!

www.ingramcontent.com/pod-product-compliance
Lightning Source LLC
Chambersburg PA
CBHW050342190726
48284CB00007BB/2121